The Extraordinary Adventures of Jake and Dogwood

The Extraordinary Adventures of Jake and Dogwood

Jean Williams

Illustrated by Mark Schofield

VANTAGE PRESS
New York

FIRST EDITION

Published by Vantage Press, Inc.
516 West 34th Street, New York, New York 10001

Manufactured in the United States of America
ISBN: 0-533-12112-4

Library of Congress Catalog Card No.: 96-90638

0 9 8 7 6 5 4 3 2 1

To my grandchildren,
Daniel and Mackenzie

Contents

The Extraordinary Adventures of Jake and Dogwood

JOURNEY TO THE WATER'S EDGE

The Arrival

The day that Jake adopted Grandma Daisy was like any other spring day. She was busy putting birdseed into the feeders in her backyard, when suddenly there was a loud squawking noise, and . . . there he was . . . out of nowhere . . . tumbling beak over tail to land a few inches from her feet.

He was a comical feather-ball, with flapping wings, and an open mouth.

"Feed me! Feed me!" he seemed to say.

Not being a bit shy, he hopped over to her on his one good leg, and squawked even louder.

"My goodness, you are hurt!" she said.

Jake didn't realize it at the time, because he was too hungry, and trying to get around with a broken leg wasn't much fun either, but he had wandered into the closest thing to bird heaven that he could have ever imagined.

She took him in and fed him, for which he was very grateful. However, putting the splint on his broken leg was another matter. He squealed and pecked as hard as he could. He struggled and squirmed with all his might. But after the feathers had settled, he hobbled across the kitchen counter with a brace on his leg made from a Band-Aid and two halves of a toothpick.

"Hmmm," he said to himself. "I guess this isn't so

bad. Actually, it feels much better!" Then he hopped into a bed she had prepared, and went to sleep.

"Coo, coo. . . ."

"Tweet, toot, toot. . . ."

"Squeak, squeak. . . ."

"Coo, Cooooooo. . . ."

"Who is making all that racket!" squawked Jake. "The sun isn't even up yet! I've had a rough life so far. I'm tired, I want to sleep!"

"Coo, my name is Dogwood. Who are you? What are you?" said a voice from the dark.

"Oh, for heaven's sake. I'm a starling, and the lady who rescued me calls me 'Jake.' Who are you, what are you, and don't you ever sleep?"

"My, aren't we cranky in the morning! Like I said, my name is Dogwood," said the voice. "I'm a dove, and I don't like to sleep when there is so much to see and do. I came to live with Grandma Daisy two years ago, when she rescued me from a family who didn't care about me anymore. How did you get here?"

"All I remember is falling out of my nest, and somehow I ended up here. So tell me, Mr. Dogwood, who else lives here?"

"Oh, many different creatures," chuckled Dogwood. "There's the rat sisters, Rhastus and Sebastian. They live in a huge glass house in the other room. Then there's the tiger finches. I can't remember all their names. They live in a big wire house and I live on top of it. Also, there's the white dove, Bernard, and

the turtle dove, Olivia. They live in a wire house in the kitchen."

"Are you sure there's enough food for everyone?" said Jake. "Speaking of food, I'm hungry. When's breakfast!"

Whoosh! Dogwood flew from his perch down to the floor. Jake followed, and stood sizing him up in the pale morning light.

Dogwood started strutting around, doing his territorial dance, like a real big shot. Jake, without much light to see, took one look at Dogwood's squiggling, pink toes, and thought he'd found himself a worm fest.

"Breakfast!" he shouted with glee, and started pecking away at those long, dancing toes.

At first, Dogwood was so surprised, he didn't know what to do. Then he became quite indignant.

"Ouch, those are my toes!" yipped Dogwood. "Back off, feather-ball!"

The News

So that is how Jake came to live with Grandma Daisy. She was a different kind of human person. She did not consider the animals to be "pets," but rather, considered herself privileged to share her place on earth with a multitude of domestic and wild creatures. They taught her respect for nature and all living things.

Several months passed, and Jake's leg was completely healed, except for a bump on the side. His

fluffy feathers had grown dark and smooth, and he was quite a handsome fellow. He spent his days poking around the house and yard. His favorite pastime was playing tricks on Dogwood. After the toe-pecking incident, they actually became very good friends.

One rainy summer morning, Jake was exploring the baskets and pottery that Grandma Daisy kept on top of the kitchen cabinet. He was bored. He had already eaten most of the dead bugs that he could excavate from the holes and cracks. Although they were completely void of any nutritional value, he considered them a great snack. Kind of like potato chips.

Dogwood was sitting on his perch. He was busy preening his white shiny feathers, looking all stately and dignified, when Jake decided it would be fun to gross him out, by pretending to swallow a rubberband. Jake swooped down on the table where Grandma Daisy kept her newspapers, and snagged one of the big green rubbery things, used to keep them in a roll. Jake, smiling to himself, landed next to Dogwood with the thing dangling from his mouth. Right away, he got the dove's attention.

If birds had eyebrows, Dogwood would have raised his. "What in the world are you doing? You're not going to eat that, are you?"

"What's the matter?" Jake mumbled with his mouth full. "Where's your sense of culinary adventure?" Just as Jake was chomping, slurping, and really getting into the sport of it, there was a loud knock at the bottom of the screen door.

"Help! Dogwood, Jake, are you there?"

"That sounds like Josephine," said Dogwood, gliding down to open the door, and hop outside.

"Phewtooey!" The green, rubbery and now slimy, thing went flying across the room. "Hey, wait for me!" yelled Jake.

Jake navigated his way through the screen door and landed with a tumble on the ground. His leg was healed, but his landings still needed a little work. He then sidestepped over to where Dogwood stood talking with two young gray squirrels, Josephine and Patches.

"Something terrible has happened!" Josephine was saying. "Opie, the possum, has journeyed up from the water's edge to find help. He told us there was dark, sticky stuff in the water, and the birds and animals are getting stuck. They need our help!"

Dogwood started jumping up and down. "What do we do? What do we do?"

His eyes opened very wide. "I'm afraid. I've never been that far from home. What if I get stuck too? Who will help us? What do we do?"

Just then Rhastus and Sebastian came climbing up from the drain pipe. "Did you hear the news?" they asked at the same time.

"What's going on?" all seventeen finches trumpeted in chorus from the inside.

Jake, who was usually the first to talk in the morning and the last to shut up at night, was now very quiet.

Finally, he said in a calm voice, "I have heard of these things from the box that Grandma Daisy listens to. I don't know for sure how they happen, but when it

does, there is great danger for all living things. Plants, birds, animals, fish, and even humans."

Dogwood gave a very undignified squawk. "What do we do!"

"I'm afraid too," replied Jake, "but we have to find a way to help. Let's begin by rounding up everyone who can go with us."

"What will Grandma Daisy say when we don't come home for dinner?" asked Sebastian, sniffling.

"You can stay here where it's safe," said Jake.

"My sister and I are going with you!" cried Rhastus, wiggling her ears. "We want to help!"

"Speak for yourself," said Sebastian. But after seeing the piercing look from her sister, she said, "Okay, okay, we want to help! But we better not get wet. I hate getting wet."

Bernard, Olivia, and the finches stayed behind to care for their young ones, and to tell Grandma Daisy about the rescue.

"Josephine, lead the way!" yelled Jake, after they gathered all the volunteers they could find, and shuffled off, by ground and treetop, toward the beach, with Dogwood taking to the air as lookout.

The Journey

That was how the rescue began. Even with the long summer days, they knew they would have to hurry to reach the water before dark.

Efforts were made to recruit help from every

creature they saw along the way. Of course, not everyone could be persuaded to join in their good deed. The crows were quite rude, and no one wanted to approach the badger in the meadow, whom Dogwood spotted from the air.

However, they were heading quite a movement of various birds and animals as they entered the park. The word traveled quickly through the animal grapevine, and more critters started joining in along the way.

There were bluejays, flickers, sparrows, raccoons, rabbits, ducks, possums, chickadees, and more joining in with each field and creek they passed. Rhastus and Sebastian got their vole cousins to join in, and all their chipmunk friends, and a few shy red squirrels.

Shortly after he entered the forest, Jake was heading down a narrow trail. He was tired from flying, and feeling a bit anxious about what faced them ahead at the beach.

Suddenly, a huge gray-and-white cat jumped in front of him and stood there towering, like the Empire State Building.

"Oh no, you don't!" squawked Jake, sounding much braver than he felt. "I didn't come all this way just to be eaten by a cat! Come near me, and I'll poke you in the eye!"

The cat smiled, sat down, and started licking the fur on his long, fuzzy tail.

"My name is Styles, and I hear you are the leader of this adventure."

"Well, . . . I guess I am," said Jake, quite astonished that he hadn't been eaten on the spot.

"I'd like to join your crusade," purred Styles, now licking his front paw.

"In a pig's eye!" blurted Jake, hoping his shaking legs wouldn't give away his fear. "You are a cat! You are a natural enemy to all of us!"

"That's true, I suppose, but I'm not your average cat." Twitching his long whiskers, he said, "I am a gentleman, a humanitarian, and I have never hurt anyone." He sat up tall and looked quite dignified.

"I have heard my friend Otto the otter, and his family are in trouble at the water," Styles continued. "I think we should all put aside our differences and help them out. What do you say?"

"Hmmm . . ." thought Jake out loud. He scratched the dirt with his toes while he was thinking. He paced around in a circle, knowing that Dogwood might have a heart attack upon seeing this huge, fearsome-looking creature. But he did appear to have a good heart, and isn't that what Grandma Daisy said we should all be judged by?

"Oh, very well," said Jake at last. "I may have trouble convincing my friends of your good intentions, but I will try."

"By the way, Mr. Styles, how do you feel about getting wet?"

The cat fidgeted a little, looked over his shoulder both ways, as if not wanting any witnesses to his weakness.

"I'm not crazy about the idea," said Styles, shrugging, and they headed on down the trail, chatting side by side.

The Pterodactyl

Meanwhile, Dogwood was flying above the trees just ahead. Not being used to long journeys, he tired easily, and decided to take a break. He searched for a safe resting place.

Ah, perfect, he thought, as he swooped down and climbed into a hole at the top of a tree that had been burned by lightning. He was just about to tuck his head under his wing for a quick snooze, when a sound came from behind.

"Phsssst!"

Dogwood jumped up and hit the top of his head. "Yikes!" he cried.

He peered back into the dark corner, still rubbing the top of his head.

"Whoa, you're different! Whhhoooo . . . what . . . who are you?" Dogwood stuttered, glancing over at the entrance and considering a speedy escape.

The creature was hanging upside down and seemed quite comfortable doing so. He had big ears, huge eyes, and funny webbed wings with no feathers on them.

"We are all different, my feathered friend. It's what you do with the difference that counts," he said, with a slight lisping sound, trying to talk around his two front teeth.

"You can embrace it, or try to change it. I personally like being different!" Then he made a jolly little squeaking noise, "Schkehee."

"My name is Sylvester and I'm a bat."

"Whewh!" Dogwood sighed. "That's a relief! For a minute there, I thought you were a tiny pterodactyl or something."

"Oh, heavens no," Sylvester giggled. "I think maybe you have been watching too many dinosaur movies!"

"Pterodactyls have been extinct for about a bizillion years," lisped the little fellow, dropping down to talk face to face.

"Besides," he continued, "bats are much more interesting. Did you know that I eat many times my weight in bugs each night?"

"Isn't that amazing." Dogwood yawned. "I would never have taken you for such a glutton."

"Schkehee!" Sylvester laughed. "Anyway, what brings you to my neighborhood?"

Dogwood took a deep breath, then explained the whole situation to his new friend, who had been sleeping all day, and wasn't aware of the tragedy going on at the beach.

Sylvester insisted on joining the rescue effort and wanted to leave right away. They flew off through the forest, in the direction of the water. Dogwood, with his smooth, gliding strokes . . . "coo, coo." Sylvester, with his choppy, flittery strokes . . . "schkehee!"

The Intruder

The weather had been misty all day, but now the wind was kicking up and the clouds were getting dark. A summer storm was brewing.

Rhastus and Sebastian were scurrying along the top of a long, steel-barred fence when it started to pour down buckets of rain.

"Oh, this is just great!" shouted Sebastian. "I'm getting wet! I hate being wet! Is it too late to turn back?"

"Don't be such a weenie! Of course it's too late to turn back. We are already halfway there. Besides, everyone is counting on us. How could we explain going back?" asked Rhastus, shaking the rain off her back.

"I don't know, but I wish I was at home, eating Grandma Daisy's casserole," replied Sebastian, bobbing her head to get water out of her ear.

"You HATE Grandma Daisy's casserole!" said Rhastus.

"I know, but it sure sounds good right now," answered Sebastian, shivering. "I'm cold, and soaking wet . . . AAAhhchewww!"

"Okay, okay. Maybe we should look for a place to dry off and wait for this downpour to stop." Rhastus looked around for shelter. "Down there!" she cried. "That looks like a nice, dry gopher hole. What do you think?"

"Gopher hole? Okay, very well. Anything to get dry again!" Then Sebastian scurried down the fence, and ran off through the wet grass.

Rhastus caught up with her at the entrance of the burrow. "Geez, I've never seen you run so fast!" she said, grabbing Sebastian's tail before she could dive into the darkness of the hole.

"Wait just a minute. What should we do if the gopher is in there?" asked Rhastus, holding tightly to her sister.

"We are rats. Rats are bigger than gophers, right?" said Sebastian. "We'll just tell him to lump it, or leave, 'cause he's got company, like it or not," she said, struggling to free herself from Rhastus's grip on her tail. "Ouch, let go!"

Rhastus let go . . .

"Schwoompp!" Sebastian disappeared into the hole.

"Ooooops!"

Rhastus dove in after her sister. As her eyes adjusted to the darkness, she called out, "Sebastian! Where are you? Mr. Gopher, are you there? Is anyone there?"

From a distance ahead, Rhastus heard Sebastian's voice calling out: "Yo, Mr. Gopher dude, are you home?"

Then she heard Sebastian squeal, "Ohhh, mercy! Let me out of here!"

"Swhiiisshhh!" came the sound as Sebastian raced past Rhastus toward the entrance, yelling, "Ahhhaaawww! Outta my way!"

"What the heck . . .?" Then Rhastus heard a noise that made the hair on her back stand straight up.

"Hhhsssssss . . ."

Then she saw a long, skinny, forked snakylike

tongue flick around the corner, "Phellewt . . . smack, smack."

Rhastus stood up on her hind legs and prepared to fight, because she realized that the snakylike tongue, was probably attached to a snakylike reptile, who'd come in to get out of the rain, as they did.

But just as the piercing green eyes, attached to the snakylike nose and the snakylike tongue, came around the corner, Rhastus had a surprising thought. *This time, my wimpy sister is right. These odds are not good . . .*

Then she turned and, "Sswwiiisshhh!" . . . she was gone too.

Sebastian was waiting outside, hiding behind a nearby tree stump. She ran to catch up with Rhastus, who was heading back toward the fence. Rain or not, they would have to continue on.

"That will teach you to go into someone else's home without being invited!" huffed Sebastian.

Back in the distance, they could hear a raspy voice. "Ssssay, girls, come back! Let'sss talk about thisssss. I'm really very nice-ssss. Phellewt . . . smack, smack!"

Bah-aaad Manners

Josephine raised her head from drinking at the creek's edge. Then suddenly, she could hear Patches up ahead, chittering out his warning cry.

What now? she thought. *He has sounded the*

alarm over every little thing. This time it is probably a piece of tin foil blowing across the trail.

Then she heard another sound.

"Wait . . . what was that?" she said out loud, straining her ears to pick up the sound again.

There it went. "Chop, chop, buzz, buzz, hack, chop."

"Oh no, not again!" She leaped into the air, and with amazing acrobatics, she jumped from tree to tree, and branch to branch.

Finally, guided by her friend's "chit chittering" sound, she shimmied down the bark of a tree, and hung by her hind legs next to him.

"Is it the same thing?" she asked, breathlessly.

"I'm afraid so!" he said, with his tail twitching above his head. "Chitter chit chitter!"

She looked down through the leaves and sure enough, there they were. The humans wearing funny orange things on their backs, and turtlelike covers on their heads. She knew they were there to level the forest and build large dwellings for their kind to live in.

Her heart sank as she thought of the forest homes that would be destroyed, and the animal lives that would be lost.

"There's nothing we can do about this," Patches said softly. Then he jumped up to the next tree. "Come on, it's getting late, we have to find a way to go around, so we can meet the others at the beach!"

Fighting back tears, Josephine sprang forward to catch the same tree, but she missed, and went

thrashing down to the ground, leaves flying everywhere, and landed with a "whomp!"

She sat up and shook her head. "I missed!" She shook her head again. "I missed! Patches, did you see that?"

"Bahaaa . . ."

Josephine flew straight up about two feet, and back down again. "You are not Patches, who are you?" she demanded, quite indignant that anyone else saw her, the most sure-footed squirrel in the forest, fall from a tree. How embarrassing!

Just then, Patches scampered up to her side. "Are you all right?"

"Yes," she said, rubbing her nose. "But I heard someone make a sound from those bushes." She nodded her head in the direction of a huge briar patch.

Patches approached the edge of the briar bushes very cautiously, one inch at a time, with his tail curled and twitching above his head.

"Who's in there!?" he chittered, ready to run at the slightest sign of danger.

"Bahaaa . . ." came the sound again.

"My name is William. The chopping noise scared me, and I ran away from my mommy, and now I'm stuck!"

No longer afraid, Patches peered into the brush in the direction of the squeaky voice. Josephine was soon at his side, squinting her eyes to see.

"It's a baby goat!" she shouted, with relief and surprise.

"You're kidding?" Patches laughed. "No pun

intended!" He laughed even harder. "Billy the goat? Oh, that's too much." Now he was in stitches, rolling on the ground.

"BAHAAA! Sniff, sniff . . . bah!"

"William, it's okay. Sorry that my friend is so insensitive," Josephine said in a soothing voice, while throwing a "shall-I-kill-you-now-or-later?" look at Patches.

"We are going to help you get out of there, and find your mother again, aren't we, Patches?" she said, narrowing her eyes at her friend, who was still lying on the ground chuckling.

Trying hard to regain his composure, Patches got up and shook himself off. With one hand on his aching side and the other poised over his mouth, in case he lost control again, he said, "Sure, sure, no problem."

They worked for almost an hour to free the young kid. The sharp thistles were a challenge, but finally he was able to stumble back out, the way he came in, and stood there facing his rescuers.

"There now, everything will be fine!" Josephine said, feeling rather heroic. "Which way do we go to find your mommy?"

"Back up the trail. Thank you so much for helping me!" bleated the young fellow, as he ran around kicking up his heels.

Just then, William's mother came sailing down the trail with her ears flopping and the bell around her neck making an incredible racket.

"Billy, Billy!" she shouted. "Are you okay?"

After a brief explanation, the two squirrels hurried

on their way, leaving the mom and son to enjoy their reunion.

The Road

Jake sat on his madrona tree perch, looking down at the most frightening spectacle he had ever seen. It was a busy road curving around the bottom of the hill. It was very noisy, and every few seconds, there were huge shiny, metal boxes on wheels that went zooming by so fast, it made the tree shake.

Styles said the beach is not far beyond this treacherous thing. Watching nervously, he thought, *Gads, how does anyone make it to the other side without getting squished flatter than a pancake!?*

I'll have to fly much higher and farther than the top of Grandma Daisy's kitchen cabinet! His muscles ached already.

He cocked his head to one side. *How do creatures without wings manage to get across safely?* His heart started beating faster.

"Oh, my goodness!" he said loud enough to be heard above the noise. He suddenly felt very protective of his friends Josephine, Patches, Rhastus, Sebastian, and all the others who had joined in their effort.

"This is as far as they go! When they get here, I will tell them to turn back. I can't be responsible for their deaths." He shivered at the thought.

Absolutely NOT! he thought firmly. *They can beg, and plead, and tell me they have done it before, but I*

will not let them go down there and make a suicide run across that moving, honking, noisy thing!

He paced up and down the tree limb, practicing the speech he would give the others when they arrived. He was concentrating so hard that he didn't notice Dogwood fly in and land behind him.

"Hi, Jake!"

"Yeeowwwh!" Jake cried with a start. "You scared me to death!"

"Sorry. Hey, I have a great new friend for you to meet. He should be along any minute," said Dogwood with excitement.

"Yeah, I have a new friend for you to meet too," Jake said, still uncertain how to tell him about Styles the cat. "But right now, we have a big problem. Look down there!" Jake pointed his wing in the direction of the road.

"The road? Yeah, so? Josephine has told me all about it," said Dogwood with a shrug and started preening the dust off his feathers.

"So! So? So they could get killed trying to run across there with all those big, noisy, fast . . . thh . . . things!" Jake stuttered, having reached quite a state of exasperation.

"Run across? Who told you that? Why would they try to run across? Ha! They would end up flatter than a pizza box. They don't run across. They go underneath through the water culvert, you silly feather-ball. Ha, ha!" said Dogwood, having a great laugh.

Jake sat there quietly, blinking his eyes for the longest time. Just as Dogwood was starting to get really

uncomfortable with the silence, Jake said, "Come on, Dogwood, old buddy. I have a new friend I would like you to meet. He is waiting down there under the picnic table. His name is Styles, and you are going to love him."

"Fabulous!" shouted Dogwood, taking flight behind his roommate. He felt relieved that Jake had recovered from his anxiety attack without saying one spiteful word. Quite unusual.

Welcome Wagon

"YEEHAW!"

Sylvester came flittering out of the culvert on the other side of the road.

YAHWHOOIE! What a trip! he thought. *It's all dark and musty in there, and it has a great echo. My kind of place!*

Oh, it's bright out here, he thought, shielding his sensitive eyes from the setting sun, which had finally come out after the passing storm.

I'm going to need my shades. He settled in a maple tree, hanging by his hind legs, and began cleaning his sunglasses.

I wonder what happened to Dogwood. I hope he found his friend, Jake. They must be somewhere up ahead. Sylvester was thinking. *The old boy travels pretty fast, even with all those feathers in the way. I better get go . . .*

"Schwunkk!"

A huge crow had landed on Sylvester's branch. With his powerful claws, he shook it so hard, the bat was catapulted out of the tree.

He curled into a ball and sailed through the air for what seemed like an eternity. Then he hit the ground with a "thump!"

Slowly, Sylvester unwrapped his wings from his head and looked around. Then he let out a nervous little "Schkehee . . ."

Standing all around him were a dozen huge, menacing crows.

"Hello!" lisped Sylvester. "I'm new in this area. I don't suppose you gentlemen are by chance, members of the Welcome Wagon?"

"CAW! Welcome Wagon? Yeah, that's right! We're members of the Welcome Wagon!" said one scruffy fellow snickering.

They all started laughing, snickering, and guffawing.

Sylvester stood up and joined in with his jolly "Schkehee-ee." He was thinking, *Maybe these chaps aren't as mean as they look.*

Then from behind: "CAW, CAW!"

"That's enough, shut up, you lame brains!" Everyone immediately became silent.

Sylvester put on his best toothy smile and turned around to greet the obvious leader of this imposing gang.

"Sir, my name is Sylvester, and I am honored to make your acquaintance." He extended his wing for a friendly shake.

"CAW-HA-HA."

"My name is Vinnie. Those are pretty cool sunglasses you have on," said the largest crow, ignoring the invitation to shake.

"Yeah, those glasses are way too cool for a scrawny little squirt like you," he said, crow-hopping up to tower over Sylvester.

"Hand'em over. Give them to me!" commanded Vinnie.

"Oh, I see . . ." said Sylvester. "Well, I don't want to give you my sunglasses, but thanks for offering to take them off my hands."

"CAW, caw, tsk, tsk, click, tsk," came the chatter.

"Let us have a little fun with him, boss," said the one with a nose ring through the top of his beak.

"Yeah, I bet he would make a great toenail buffer!" cawed in another.

"Gulp." Sylvester noticed the circle tightening toward him.

"Mr. Vinnie, I have reconsidered." He looked up at the burly fellow. "You may have my sunglasses. They might fit a little tight, but you can get them . . . yikes!"

The huge crow had picked Sylvester up by the back of his ears. His yellow eyes glared at the frightened, shaking, little bat.

"TOO LATE!" he cawed and dropped Sylvester into the waiting wings of the gang. "Let's have some fun!"

Just then, an ear-piercing siren whistle rang out across the forest. They all stopped and looked up.

Jake was leaning against a tree, at the edge of the

clearing, feeling quite proud of his minah-like ability to imitate shrill sounds.

"You know, Grandma Daisy always said that only bullies have to fight. Isn't that right, Dogwood?"

"Yep!" came the reply from the opposite direction. The crows turned their heads to follow the sound. "Bullies and cowards!" yelled Dogwood.

"Hi, guys!" shouted Sylvester, as he jumped up to join his friends.

"NOT SO FAST!" snarled Vinnie, and with one sweep of his powerful wing, he sent Sylvester sprawling to the feet of the other crows.

Then he turned to glare at the pests that were interrupting the fun. "Caw, ha-ha!" he trumpeted. "A puny starling, and a whimpy dove are going to stop us? Just how do you plan to do that? Caw-ha! Do you have an army of alligators hiding in the trees?"

The gang joined in. "Cah hee hee, snicker, chuckle! That's funny, boss! Ha ha!"

"Not just a starling and a dove," Jake shouted above the roar.

But they kept on laughing and started shoving Sylvester from side to side.

"HOW ABOUT A CAT?" asked Dogwood, swooping down over their heads. "A huge cat, with sharp claws, and very long teeth!"

Everyone froze and looked around slowly.

"Oh, sure!" growled Vinnie. "A dove and a starling hanging out with a ferocious cat!" He pointed his wing. "You almost had us going!"

"Caw ha." Then, just as everyone was starting to have another good laugh . . .

"Whoosh." Styles lunged into the clearing. "Actually, that about sums it up!"

"Holy moly, a cat! We're dead! We're dead!" They all started tripping over each other.

Then Styles held up his paw for all to see. He raised his eyebrows and twitched his whiskers.

"Ping!" came the sound, as he flicked up one awesome claw. "Ping, ping." Another and then another.

Whines, whimpers and . . . "outta my way!" Voices started squeaking out, as the feathers flew.

"Move, move, move!"

"Ouch, you stepped on my toe, you slug!"

"Flap, flap, whoosh," came the sound, as they all scattered.

Finally, when the dust had settled, all the bad guys were gone.

There was just Sylvester, still wearing his sunglasses, and his new friends, Jake, Dogwood, and Styles . . .

All prancing around, hugging, and giving each other the high sign.

The History Lesson

Rhastus had only visited the water's edge once, with her mother when she was very young. That was long before she and Sebastian were orphaned and came to live with Grandma Daisy.

She sat on a mossy rock, once again overlooking the vast blue-green water. It was more beautiful than she remembered. The golden sparkles shimmered and danced off the waves, as the setting sun paid its final tribute to the day.

They had made good time after leaving the gopher burrow, and she was quite sure they were the first rescuers to arrive.

Sebastian was busy in a nearby elderberry field, regaining her strength by eating everything in sight.

Yek, how can she eat at a time like this? thought Rhastus, feeling a bit queasy.

She sat at full attention, with her front paws stretched forward, ears alert, and her nose raised to the breeze. She had been using all her senses to find signs of trouble, but she had found nothing.

Sure hope someone isn't playing a cruel joke on all of us! she was thinking, when . . .

Above the gentle swooshing sound of the waves, Rhastus caught the sound of Sebastian's unmistakable cry for help.

Oh, please! she thought, springing forward in the direction of her sister's caterwauling. *Scorpions, poison traps, porcupines, . . . anything but another snake!*

With lightning speed, Rhastus covered the distance to her sister in a matter of minutes. From the wailing and screeching, she expected to find a scene of bloody torture. Instead, what she came upon, was Sebastian hanging upside down, with her ankle caught in a massive net.

"What the heck are you doing up there?" quipped Rhastus, relieved, but fighting hard not to laugh.

"I'm trying out for the circus trapeze! What do you think I'm doing up here?" squeaked Sebastian, sarcastically. "GET ME DOWN!"

"Okay, okay, keep your toes on!" Rhastus chuckled. She scrambled up the bush to the edge of the net, wrapped her tail around a twig for balance, and scoped out her sister's situation.

"Couldn't resist the fat, juicy ones at the top, huh?"

"These stupid nets are supposed to keep birds out!" squirmed Sebastian. "Do I look like a bird!"

"Be still!" ordered Rhastus. "You've gotten yourself tied up pretty good. I can't seem to undo this knot!"

"Chew it with your teeth!"

"What do you think I'm trying to do!" shouted Rhastus, between nibbles. "Gnaw, gnaw! This stuff is made from leather-laced cement, or something!"

"Please, allow me," came a voice with a well-groomed accent.

The sisters swiveled their heads toward the intruder. "Ah, ah, Rhastus, . . . I think . . . ah, isn't that a ferret?" whispered Sebastian.

"The problem is her body weight!" stated the aristocratic, weasellike fellow.

"I beg your pardon!" miffed Sebastian.

"What I mean is . . ." he said, removing his glasses for a quick cleaning, to have a better look at the situation. "In order to successfully chew through her bindings, I must hold her up, so the tension on the

plexy-polyurethane fibers will be reduced." He reached up to demonstrate.

"Phffst! Don't you touch me!" hissed Sebastian.

"Oh, my apologies, madame!" said the ferret, retracking himself quickly. "You are correct, of course," lowering his head to make a polite bow. "Allow me to properly introduce myself.

"My name is Daggot Zipper the third." He readjusted his glasses. "My family have been caretakers of these grounds for many generations."

"So then, you are a ferret, are you not?" asked Rhastus.

"Yes, that is correct," replied Mr. Zipper III, with enthusiasm.

"Well," said Rhastus. "If I remember Grandma Daisy's history lessons, ferrets were once used by humans to help hunt down poor little rabbits and innocent little rats. Isn't that true?"

"Ah, history! My best subject!" boasted Mr. Zipper, oblivious to her scornful tone. "Actually, my great, great, great-grandfather was a European polecat. Can you imagine that?" Zipper chuckled, quite amused with it all.

"You didn't answer my sister's question," Sebastian wiggled. "If you are going to eat us, do it soon, because my foot is killing me!"

"Eat you? What a ghastly thought!" shouted Zipper, grimacing. "Generations of training and education have taught us a more civilized way to exist," he said, with pride.

"Now, if you two have decided that you do not

need my assistance, FINE!" said the indignant fellow. "I have more important things to do." Then he turned, and scurried off, with his short legs moving so rapidly, they could barely be seen. Rhastus looked down at Sebastian. Sebastian craned her neck to look up at Rhastus.

"Could be worse," said Rhastus. "Could be a snake." Silence . . .

"Oh yoo-hoo! Mr. Zipper, sir!" they called after him. "Maybe you could share more of your family history, while helping us get out of this mess. Come on, what do you say?"

"Clever girls!" responded Zipper, shuffling back into the area. "Thought you might see it my way. Where should I begin?" he said, reaching up to support Sebastian, while Rhastus chewed away. "Oh yes, it all began in pre-historic times . . .

The Oil Spill

Later that evening, at the water's edge, down around the jetty, there was an incredible gathering of creatures.

Different birds and animals of major diversity had gathered to respond to the enormous need of help for all the beach and water wildlife.

A heavy silence had fallen over the "Grandma Daisy" group.

Jake, Dogwood, Styles, and Sylvester had joined up with Josephine and Patches. The last to join the group were Rhastus and Sebastian, who finally

managed to break away from Mr. Zipper's history lesson, and hurry back to the beach.

After a jubilant reunion and some introductions, they had become very quiet and were now focusing on the activity at the water.

There were humans aboard floating vessels out in the distance. They had flashing lights, and many voices could be heard.

Dark blotches dotted the rocks on shore. Heavy shadows seemed to bob and float atop the incoming waves.

"What do you suppose it is?" asked Styles, breaking the silence.

"It's called oil!" said Rhastus.

"Yeah . . . oil," piped in Sebastian.

"Oil? How do you know?" asked Josephine. Then she turned to Patches and whispered, "What's oil?"

"They are right," said Jake, remembering something he had heard at home. "It's thick and gooey, like the syrup Grandma Daisy puts on our Sunday pancakes."

"Ahhh," they all replied, nodding their heads with understanding. But mostly they were thinking of those delicious pancakes.

"Why would it be in the water?" asked Dogwood, quite confused.

"Because the humans carry it in their floating vessels," explained Rhastus, quite certain of herself.

"If one crashes, the oil can sometimes leak into the water!"

"That's right!" agreed Sebastian.

"Geez, how did you two get so smart all of a sudden?" cracked Patches, with his usual lack of diplomacy.

"Mr. Zipper told us," said Rhastus.

"Yeah," chimed in Sebastian. "He's the caretaker of the elderberry fields over that hill." She nodded her head in that direction. "We met him today, while . . . ahem . . . eating dinner."

"He knows everything that goes on down here," said Rhastus.

"Does he know how these awful accidents happen?" asked Sylvester, flittering forward from his driftwood perch. "I mean . . . how could humans let this happen? Aren't they supposed to be smarter than anyone?"

"HELP ME!" came a faint voice down by the shore rocks. "Help my baby, please!"

"Mrs. Otter!" shouted Styles, as he leaped forward.

His fear of water forgotten, Styles jumped and splashed through the messy water, until he reached the place where Mrs. Otter was standing over her shivering baby.

He could see that the little one was matted with thick oil. "How can I help, old girl?"

"Styles, is that you?" asked Mrs. Otter, wiping tears from her eyes, so she could see better.

"Yes, I'm here," he said, putting a paw around her shoulder. "Where is Mr. Otter?"

"GONE!" she cried. "He pushed our young one to the shore, then he disappeared. I'm afraid he is dead."

Her eyes filled with tears and sadness. "But now, I have to save our baby. Please help me!"

"WHAT SHOULD WE DO?" came a chorus of voices from all the creatures who had moved forward, in response to her cries.

"I don't know how to get this nasty stuff off her fur," said Mrs. Otter, sniffing. "It weighs her down, she can't swim, and she is losing her body warmth!"

Jake and Dogwood watched from a nearby sand dune. They could see the young otter was barely moving, and her eyes were closed.

"We have to think of something quick, or she will die," whispered Jake.

"Maybe we could use the fluffy cottonwood tuffs to wipe it off," suggested Dogwood.

"Whoo . . . that wouldn't be wise," said a majestic spotted owl, swooping down to join them.

"Why not?" they both asked.

"It would stick to the oil and make the problem worse," said the owl, still blinking to adjust his eyes to the remaining twilight.

"My name is Chesterfield, and I was here when this happened once before a few years ago," he said, swiveling his head. "It was a major disaster. Many lives were lost. But this time, I have an idea.

"I think the most important thing is to reach everyone who needs help as quickly as possible," he continued. "We must hurry!"

Jake and Dogwood had been joined by a rather large group of rescuers who were eager to help.

"Tell us what to do! She is dying!!" they yelled in unison.

"Okay, first we will need to drench her with elderberry juice," said the owl, swiveling his head. "It has a natural acid that will help break down the stickiness of the oil and make it easier to wipe off.

"Second, we will need someone to dig up plenty of soft, moist sand to pack on her body after we put on the berry juice," said the wise old owl, with the voice of experience.

"The sand will act as a poultice and will draw the oil with it, when it's wiped off. Quick, we must hurry now!"

"Okay, I'm your man for digging," said Zipper, scampering in from the shadows.

"Mr. Zipper, what are you doing here?" asked Rhastus and Sebastian.

"You don't think I would miss all the fun, do you?" he said and started digging furiously. Sand flew high into the air, as his head quickly disappeared and he became engulfed by his work.

"Now for the problem of getting the elderberry juice. We are running out of time," said the owl, "and believe me, there will be many more who will need the same treatment!"

"If we turn back the nets, our feathered friends can pluck the elderberries and form a rotation line," suggested Rhastus. "They can fly in a circle, swooping down to squeeze out the juice, then go back for more."

"Good idea!" shouted the owl and flew off toward the elderberry fields, followed by most of the others.

Jake, Dogwood, and Styles formed another group to go out in search of stranded birds and animals, who might also need their help.

The Bagpipe

That night, as the work continued, a full moon gradually rose over the water. The pale light was a great advantage, especially for the birds, who were not accustomed to flying in darkness.

It was an incredible sight. There were hundreds of birds flying in a giant circle, lead by Chesterfield, and followed by rufus-sided towhees, blue jays, robins, finches, sparrows, warblers, kinglets, thrushes, wrens, chickadees, nuthatches, grosbeaks, tiny little hummingbirds, huge red-tailed hawks, and many more.

They were taking turns swooping down over the uncovered bushes, plucking a few elderberries, then flying down to squeeze the juice over the oil-covered victims, who had come seeking help. There were injured ducks, otters, beavers, herons, egrets, kingfishers, mollusks, and snails, to name a few.

Another team of rescuers were using clam shells to carry Zipper's moist sand, and pack it over the oil- and juice-covered critters. Then later, the entire mess was wiped off with a cottonwood bundle, allowing the creature to start cleaning, and healing itself.

Meanwhile, back at the sand dunes, Zipper peaked up over the edge. There were piles of moist sand, as far as the eye could see. He had gotten help from several

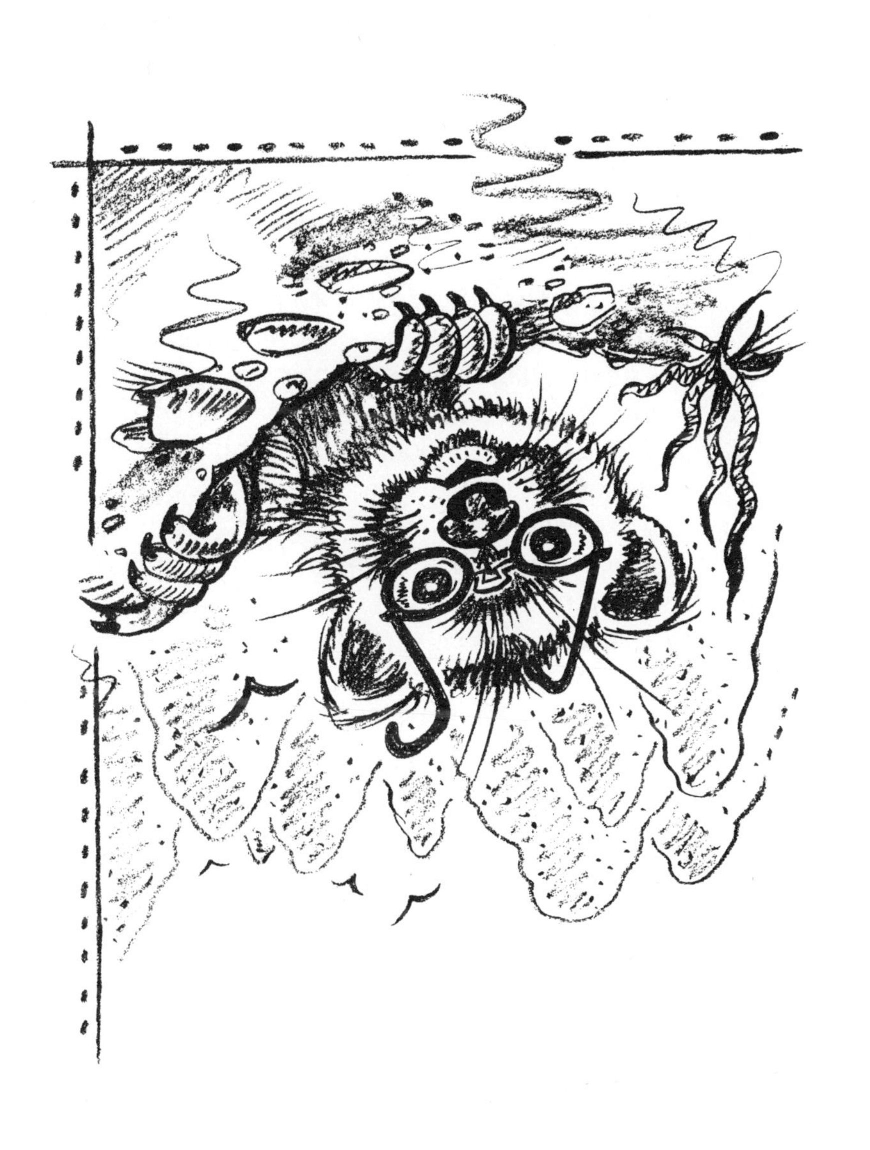

squirrel, raccoon, and rat rescuers, who were also skilled diggers.

Time for a break, he thought, shaking his weary head.

Sand went flying everywhere. He cleaned his glasses and looked around. “This rescue business is hard work. I need to take a walk and stretch my legs. Hhmmm . . . where should I go to be out of the way?”

Then he heard sneezing and cooing sounds coming from the next dune."Ah, I’ll go over and see how Dogwood is doing with the cottonwood bundles."

“Coo-coo-waa-coo,” said Dogwood. His throat billowed out, as if he had swallowed a balloon.

“Hey, old chum, your neck is all swollen up!” shouted Zipper, as he appeared at the top of the hill. “Is it painful? Do you need help? Are you choking?”

“What?” asked Dogwood. His neck was skinny again, and he looked surprised by Zipper’s concern.

“Good grief, how do you do that?” Zipper shuffled over to Dogwood, for a closer inspection.

“I don’t know.” Dogwood shrugged. “I guess I just hold a lot of air in my throat, and blow it out to make my cooing sounds.”

“Like a bagpipe!” exclaimed Zipper, with fascination.

“Ahh . . . ahhh . . . ahchewww!” sneezed Dogwood, blowing a throat full of air at the curious ferret. The force blew Zipper backwards, and he tumbled, head over tail, down the sandy hill.

“I’m so sorry!” shouted Dogwood, flying down to

pull Zipper's head out of the sand, and help him get on his stubby, little feet.

"Phewst! Phewtooey!" Zipper spit out a mouthful of sand. Then, using his front paws, he wiped the sand off his ears and whiskers. "That was interesting."

"Sorry, I have been sneezing all night!" apologized Dogwood. "I don't know how I got chosen to do the cottonwood bundling. It turns out that I am quite allergic."

"Well, I heard it was your brilliant idea to use the cottonwood tuffs," said Zipper admiringly. "Lucky it's in season, and piled up in every crack, crevice, and corner. Quite ingenious, really."

"Well . . . sniff . . . I suppose it was pretty creative," said Dogwood, wiping his nose on the edge of his wing, and feeling much better. He picked up a dried blade of grass and began bundling another handful of the white, fluffy stuff.

"Alrighty then, I must get back to my digging," said Zipper, waving good-bye, as he scampered up the hill, still shaking sand out of his ears.

The Patient

"Yikes! In coming!"

Patches dropped his cottonwood bundle and threw himself flat out on the sand, with his paws over his head.

"SWOOWIISSHHH!"

A huge band-tailed pigeon missed him by inches. Patches looked up to see the bird's bright yellow claws

pass overhead. They were covered with dark elderberry juice from a recent squeeze and made quite a horrifying sight.

"That was close," muttered Patches, getting up to dust off the sand. "Close enough to see that he needs to clip his toenails. Sure glad he's on our side."

"Yeah, I know what you mean," said Josephine, using her cottonwood bundle to rub the gooey poultice off the wing of a nearby seagull.

"The first time he flew over after dropping his juice, I almost fainted!" She rolled her eyes back in her head. "It was scary."

"Almost as scary as falling out of a tree, I'll bet. Ha!" teased Patches.

"Hey, guys, I could use some help over here!" called Styles.

They saw that he had about a dozen, oil-splotched sand crabs hanging to his furry side. He gently lay down on the beach, so they could tumble off and get in line for treatment.

Josephine and Patches hopped over to their new feline friend. "Hi, Styles, how's it going out there?"

"I think we have rounded up almost everyone who needs help," he said, still lying on the ground.

"I'll bet you are tired," said Josephine, reaching for the water bucket, to offer him a drink.

"It does feel good to get off my feet for a minute. But actually, I have another patient hanging from my other side." He nodded his head back over his shoulder.

They took a peek. "Sylvester!"

He was hanging by his back feet, looking quite sticky and miserable.

He managed to squeak out a feeble little "schkehee," before sliding down to the sand.

They rushed over to help get him to the treatment line.

"He'll be okay, won't he?" asked Styles, following behind. "After carrying him on my back for half a mile, I've grown quite fond of the little fellow."

"He should be alright," said Patches. "What happened? We have all been so careful not to get caught in that awful stuff."

"It was my fault," said Styles, thinking back. "Not wanting to get wet. I asked him to fly out along the surf, to look for creatures who might need help."

"Sounds reasonable," said Josephine, who had come back, after making sure that Sylvester was juiced and packed with sand. "It will be another hour before we can remove the poultice. He's resting now."

"Go on, Styles, tell us what happened," Patches said, lying down on a grassy spot to listen.

"Well, I'm not entirely sure." Styles seemed to be thinking out loud. "From what I can figure, bats don't see very well. They use a type of radar, to keep from running into things.

"He was just offshore, when he heard the sand crabs in distress."

Styles continued, "He started calling my name, and flying low over the water, heading in my direction, trying to hear where I was.

"He was searching for me to come and help, when

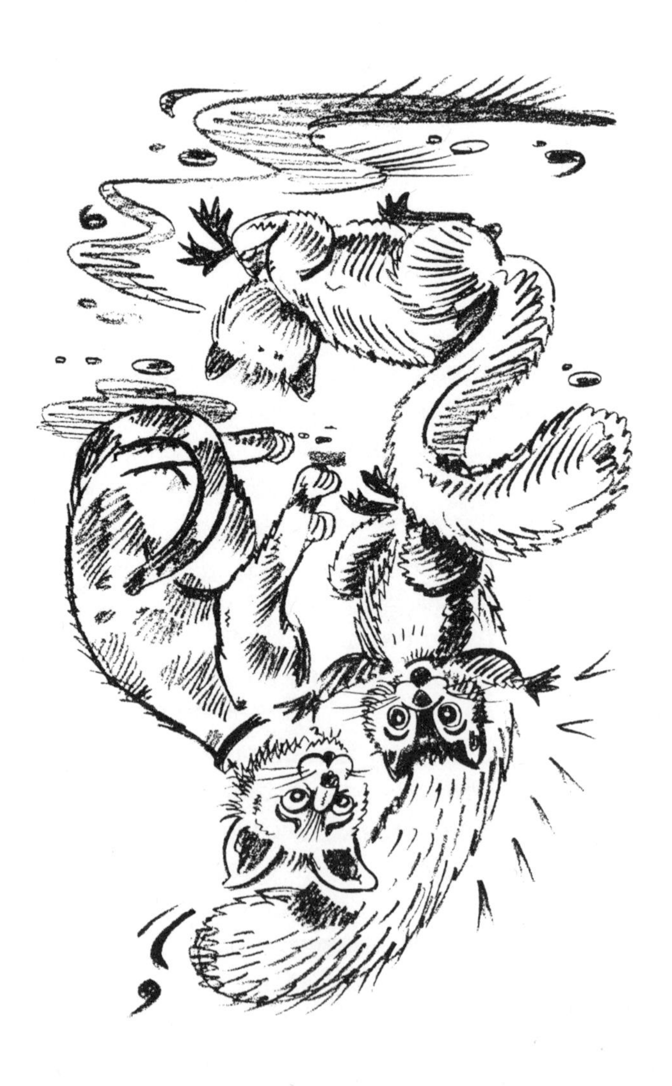

a wave seemed to just reach up and grab him," said the cat, shaking his head. "I was close enough to pull him out within seconds, but he was instantly covered with oil that must have been floating on the water. I loaded everyone up and came here."

Back at the treatment line, Dogwood found his friend and hunkered down to keep him company until the poultice could be removed. "I heard you were here," said Dogwood, sounding very concerned. "What were you thinking?"

"Styles and I saved all those sand crabs," lisped Sylvester, with his wings plastered down to his sides. "Styles got oil on his fur from carrying us here, and I got wrapped up like a taco, but it was worth it." He wiggled and said, "Scratch my nose, would you? It itches, and I can't reach it."

"Okay," said Dogwood, reaching over to dab Sylvester's pink nose with the tip of a feather. "But you have to be careful. You are not a pterodactyl, you know!"

"Schkehee!"

Sunday Pancakes

It was a glorious sunrise. The distant trees and hills were framed with a glowing crimson, pinkish color.

Chesterfield had called a gathering on the cliff top. The last of the injured had been wiped clean, and it was now time for everyone to say their thanks and farewells.

It was truly a magnificent sight. Hundreds and

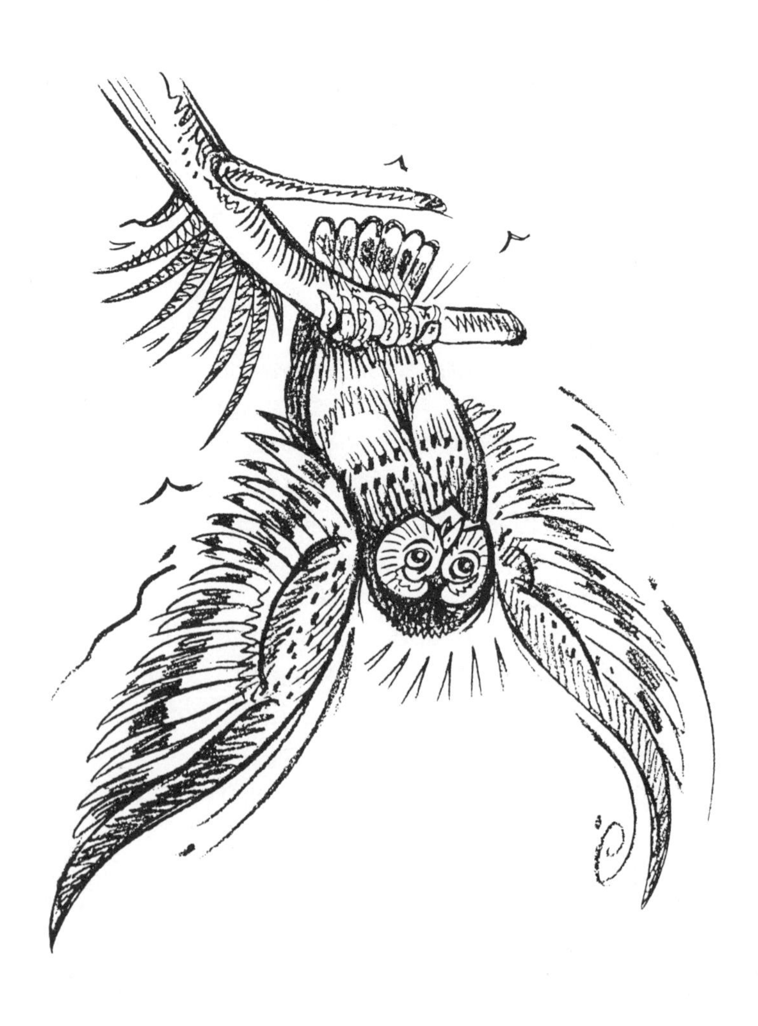

hundreds of different birds, animals, and crustaceans dotted the rocks and trees.

The Grandma Daisy group met up on a huge rock closest to the water. They sat, lay, and slouched together, completely exhausted.

"Cappucino, light on the foam," mumbled Jake.

Styles swished his tail across Jake's face. "Wake up! You are talking in your sleep."

"Ah, sorry," said Jake, yawning broadly. "There's never an espresso stand around when you need one."

Then Chesterfield glided up to the highest treetop. He held his wings outstretched above the crowd. He looked around and blinked, as if he were searching for the right words.

"BE PROUD! . . . Be very proud of what you have done here, this day!"

He looked slowly across the beach and water, then took to the air in an easterly direction. "Safe journey home to you all!"

The crowd slowly started moving away, then a great cheering, chirping, whistling, and stomping sound came together. They were celebrating each other and the miracle they had been a part of.

The group stood together, waving good-bye to Zipper, who was headed back to his elderberry fields.

"We want to thank you all for saving our baby's life," called out Mrs. Otter, as she approached them.

"Good to see you!" said Styles, rushing forward to greet her. "I heard the young one was out of danger, then things got so busy."

"How is she doing?" asked Rhastus.

"Quite well, thank you," came a strange voice beyond the rocks.

"Otto?" called Styles, raising his eyebrows, and looking at Mrs. Otter. She was smiling, with tears glistening in her eyes.

Just then, he stepped out to greet them, leading the young one by her hand. "Styles, old friend, how can I ever thank you?"

"You're not dead!" shouted Styles, suddenly alive with energy. "We thought you were a goner! How did you survive?"

"The humans saved me, and many others. I owe them my life," said Otto, pulling his wife and daughter in for a hug.

Then, they all circled around, chattering at once. Laughing, hugging, and crying.

They talked together for more than an hour, sharing stories and experiences. Then, the otter family said their tearful good-byes and headed down the beach to find a new home.

The group stood on the cliff, taking one last look at the deserted landscape and the foul mess of oil remaining on the beach. They knew it would be a long time before any wildlife could make their homes there again. But as long as creatures and humans were working to protect the environment for all, there would be hope for the future.

"Hey!" yelled Dogwood. "What day of the week is this?"

They all looked at each other, trying to remember.

"Tuesday?" suggested Patches. "I've lost track."

"No, no, it's . . ." started Jake.

"SUNDAY!" they all chorused in. "Pancakes!"

"Yeah!" exclaimed Jake, regaining energy. "If we leave now, and hurry, we could get home just in time for breakfast!"

"But what about Styles and Sylvester?" asked Sebastian, thinking of someone else besides herself, for a change.

"They can come too," said Rhastus. "Grandma Daisy won't mind!"

Sylvester hopped up to sit between Styles's ears. "Great!" he yelled. "How about a ride?"

Jake and Dogwood had already started toward home. They looked at each other, then yelled back . . .

"Yeehaw! . . ."

"LAST ONE THROUGH THE CULVERT IS A ROTTEN FEATHER-BALL!"

THE LOST FALCON

The Milk Man

"Dogwood!"

"Phssst, wake up!"

Jake flew across the room, barely visible in the morning light, and landed next to Dogwood on his perch. Dogwood was still snoozing, with his beak tucked under his wing. Jake leaned over and yelled, "Wake up, the milk man is outside!"

"What! What!" Dogwood jumped up, then sat squinting at his friend. "The milk man? He's here every Monday. What's the big deal? Hey, you're not coming down with the tropical fever again, are you?"

"No, don't you remember our plan?" Jake said, poking Dogwood with his wing tip to jog his memory. "ICE CREAM."

"Oh yeah." Dogwood yawned, scratching his head. "Tell me the plan again."

"We fly into the truck while Mr. Walter is making his delivery to Grandma Daisy and sneak out with some goodies," explained Jake.

"That's the plan?" Dogwood shrugged. "Sounds like stealing to me. Grandma Daisy won't like it."

"He can add it to her bill later. Come on, don't be a wimp!" cried Jake. "My birthday is coming up. You know she gives us whatever we want for our birthday. I

just want it a little early, that's all. Come on, we have to hurry."

"I don't know, this doesn't sound too bright to me," said Dogwood, trying to be sensible. "What if we get caught?"

Jake flew over to the kitchen window. "You know, you're probably right. It's not worth the risk. Grandma Daisy has had us on this high-protein diet for a month now. Actually, I'm starting to LIKE tofu rolled in sunflower seeds and oatmeal."

"Ugh, yuk," sputtered Dogwood, covering his mouth with his wing. "Please, let's not think about that so early in the morning."

"No kidding!" said Jake. "I would much rather think about french vanilla, rocky road, or cookies and cream!"

"Cookies and cream?" said Dogwood, dreaming out loud. "Okay, let's go for it! How do we get in there?"

Jake could see that Mr. Walter had loaded up Grandma Daisy's crate and was headed around to the back porch to make his delivery.

"Follow me!" yelled Jake, as he squeezed through the opening at the kitchen window. "Good thing Grandma Daisy likes fresh air."

Jake swooped through the door of the milk truck and landed on a huge egg carton.

"Ice cream, popsicles, sweet stuff, where are you?" called Jake. "Come to Poppa!" He flew over to a glass container that looked promising.

"Whoa!" he said, skidding over to the edge. "This is slippery."

DAIRY
EGGS
EGGS
MILK
MILK

Just then Dogwood came swhooshing in. "You didn't leave much room for me to get out of that window!"

"Oh, yeah?" teased Jake. "Maybe you SHOULD lose some weight! . . . Hey, don't land here, it's slippery!"

But Jake's warning came to late. Dogwood touched down on the frosty glass lid and started skidding across the top. "Whoa, yikes!"

Jake tried to move out of the way, but the only thing that moved was his feet, slipping back and forth.

"LOOK OUT!" yelled Dogwood, as he bowled Jake over, and they both toppled to the floor.

"Ow!" whined Jake. "You made me lose a tail feather. Do you know how long it takes for my tail feathers to grow back!"

"Sorry," said Dogwood, shaking himself to see if there was any damage. "But you looked pretty funny moving those stubby toes so fast. Why didn't you just fly out of my way?"

"Oh sure!" said Jake mockingly. "Why didn't you just fly out of my way!"

"Sshhhh . . . someone is coming!" whispered Dogwood.

They both stumbled over to peek around the edge of the container. Just then, the heavy truck door was pulled shut.

"Ah . . . oops. I think we are in trouble," came Jake's voice from the darkness.

Then the engine started up and the milk truck drove away . . . with Jake and Dogwood trapped inside.

Fudgesicles

"Hey, Penny, it's you again on television!"

The old black lab was pointing his nose toward the TV screen displayed in a nearby store window.

"Geez, you are a celebrity. Can I have your autograph?" He chuckled.

"Really? Let me see!" came a voice from somewhere over the rooftop.

"Swhoosh!" The graceful bird glided down to land near the old pooch, who was lying next to his favorite fire hydrant.

"Well, Sparky, I guess I am getting pretty famous. That makes twice this week I have been on the evening news." She giggled as they watched the program. "You would think they have never seen a Peregrine falcon before!"

"Not many these days," said the old dog, sounding a little sad. "When I was a young pup on the farm, there were hawks and falcons hunting from every tree and fence post. Now, there are many of those families that are almost gone!

"Besides," he said, pausing to scratch behind his ear, "you were born in a nest on top of the highest building, in one of the largest cities in the world!" He stopped to scratch the other ear. "You are the only one in your family to survive the dangers of living in the city. That makes you pretty special."

"Oh heck, that's nothing!" she said modestly. "Last week I heard about a pair of spotted owls who made

their nest on top of a shopping mall, somewhere in a place called Oregon."

"A shopping mall!?" said Sparky. "That's quite a change of scenery from living in old trees, far away from humans. But you have to admit, the french fries would be better!"

"Yeah, I guess so." Penny giggled, thinking of her favorite city food. "But it is amazing where we will try to make our homes when there are few choices."

"True," said Sparky, standing up to shake off the city dust. "Just look at me, a country mutt, living here on the streets!"

"What about that?" asked the young falcon, flying up to a nearby telephone pole. "How did you end up here?"

"Last year my human family lost their farm, and I ran away from the animal shelter," explained Sparky, sounding quite proud of his escape.

"Now I live here." Sparky circled his head to indicate the streets around him. "By the way, this is one of my favorite places to get food. They make cheese and ice cream over there," he said, nodding toward a large building at the end of the block.

Just then, Mr. Walter's truck backed up to the loading dock of the building Sparky was talking about.

"Yeehaw! Follow me!" Sparky jumped up, suddenly spry and eager. "Have you ever tasted fudgesicles? Come on!"

Mr. Walter walked to the rear of his truck and started talking to some men standing on the platform. Shortly afterward, they all went inside the building.

Jake and Dogwood, still trapped inside, could hear the voices outside, and knew their chance for escape was near.

"Do you think I have time for one more eskimo pie?" came Jake's voice in the darkness. "On second thought," he said, pushing away several empty wrappers, "I think I've had enough."

"Yeah, me too," said Dogwood, taking one last peck at a popsicle stick. "Let's move forward, and get ready to fly out. They have to open that door soon!" He started feeling his way. "Come on, Jake, get ready!"

Sparky had crept close to the loading dock and sat hiding underneath it in the shadows. He knew that the men had gone inside to bring out fresh supplies for the truck, and they would be back soon. After they came out, they would open the truck door, then go back inside for a second load. There would be just enough time to dash inside the truck and retrieve a mouthful of fudgesicles.

"Are you crazy!?" Penny was trilling from the safe distance of her telephone pole.

"Sshhh . . ." Sparky whispered. He could hear the footsteps of the men overhead. He heard the metallic door of the truck open and the thumping sound of boxes being dropped inside. Then the footsteps went back into the building.

"Okay, it's now or never! Yeehaw!"

The old dog lunged forward toward the truck door. But just as he was landing on the back step, he was met by flapping wings, feathers flying, screeching noises, and two sets of big, blinking birdie eyeballs.

"Yeow!" cried Sparky, but it was too late to avoid the collision.

The white flapping feather-ball bounced off to the left, and the dark flapping feather-ball bounced off to the right. Then they both tumbled beak over tail into the shadows under the platform.

"What the heck was that?" yelled Sparky, shaking his head, and rubbing his nose.

"Are you alright!?" Penny swooped down to land on his back.

"Yeah, but hold on tight. We better scram before the men come back!" Then he darted under the platform, with the falcon clinging to his back.

"Darn, no fudgesicles today!"

Horse Sense

"Hello, Jake!" said Jake. "You're looking a little peaked this morning, Jake!"

Jake was leaning over the water at the lake's edge, talking to his reflection, while quenching his morning thirst. He and Dogwood had spent a restless night on a willow branch, in the park.

"Could it be that a huge, black beast almost gave you a heart attack yesterday?" Jake continued talking to himself.

Then, just as he caught movement in the lake's reflection, there came a loud honking and flapping noise, as a huge flock of Canadian geese swooped down to land on the small lake.

"Look out!" Startled, Jake stumbled backward, then flew up to land next to Dogwood.

"Did you see that!?" Jake asked Dogwood. "Those guys are huge! They almost knocked me into the lake."

"Too bad they didn't. You could really use a bath, you know," teased Dogwood, preening his feathers after his earlier dip in the water.

"They didn't mean any harm!" called Penny, the falcon, as she flew in to land next to the newcomers. "This is where they spend their days hunting for food."

"Hi, I'm Penny," she explained, after seeing their puzzled looks. "My friend Sparky and I didn't get a chance to talk to you yesterday after you . . . ah . . . ran into each other at Mr. Walter's truck.

"Are you fellas okay?" she asked.

Jake and Dogwood looked at each other and shrugged. "Oh, we're just dandy," said Jake, feeling uneasy, but trying to sound cocky. "Actually, what we really want is to go home. Can you help us do that?"

"I'm not sure, but I'll do my best," she replied. "Tell me where you live."

They talked together for most of the morning. Jake and Dogwood told Penny about Grandma Daisy, and all their extended animal family at home.

"I was born here in the city," said Penny. "So, I don't know about the countryside that you're speaking of."

"No way!" said Dogwood in disbelief. "I thought falcons could only live in fields and forests."

"That's where we should be," she said simply. "The problems are complicated. I don't understand it all. But

I know that only a few falcons remain. We do what we can to survive, and sometimes that includes being forced to make our home in unusual places.

"My parents made their nest on that building," she continued, pointing to a distant outline of city buildings. "There, the tallest one."

"WOW!" Jake whistled.

"That's great!" exclaimed Dogwood. "You and your family will be all right, then."

"Not exactly." She lowered her head, and spoke softly. "These are not our natural surroundings. Because of things called automobiles and windows, my parents and brother did not survive."

Her words added to their sad, homesick feeling.

"Penny girl. That is YOU up there, eh?" A strange voice broke the awkward silence.

"EDISON!" squealed the falcon with delight. She swooped down to land next to a majestic goose. "Where have you been!" she squealed again and started darting around him.

"My, my . . . settle down, child." He was obviously glad to see her too. "Theodora has been out looking for her next year's nesting ground, and I have been staying close to the young ones."

"Edison, I want you to meet my new friends, Jake and Dogwood." The newcomers didn't need much encouragement to fly down and join in the jumping and twirling. Just for the fun of it.

They learned that Edison and Theodora had become something like Penny's adoptive parents. They

learned that Penny was well known in the city, and loved by all, because of her family's tragic plight.

They also learned that there seemed to be little advice available to help them get home.

Later that afternoon, Jake and Dogwood said farewell to Edison and Penny. They knew that the best way home was to keep moving and talking to anyone who might be able to help.

"We're going home! I don't care if we have to fly all the way there!" huffed Jake, flying over the park tree tops.

"I sure hope that won't be necessary!" panted Dogwood, a short distance behind. "Wait for me!"

"Try to keep up!" Jake yelled back. "It's not my fault that doves aren't as fast as starlings."

"Maybe so, but doves are prettier!" called Dogwood, flying a little faster. "Jake, slow down. Have you forgotten that we don't know where we are going? What if we are headed in the wrong direction? I don't want to go home by way of the North Pole!"

"Okay, maybe we should try harder to get help," Jake replied, circling down to look for likely prospects.

"What the heck is that?" asked Dogwood, as they landed side by side on a park bench.

"THAT is a horse," replied Jake, remembering Grandma Daisy's TV box at home.

"Excuse me?" said a gigantic creature standing close by. She turned her head and twitched her tail. "I'm not just a horse. I am a POLICE horse, and you can call me Ms. Police Horse." Then she snorted, laughed, and stomped the ground.

"Police? Fantastic!" squawked Jake. "Then, you can help us get home, right?"

"Sure, sonny," whinnied the mare. "I know every inch of this city. Which way do you live?"

"Well, . . ." started Dogwood, throwing a doubtful look at Jake.

"We don't live in the city," continued Jake, still sounding hopeful. "We live in the country with Grandma Daisy. Do you know what direction that would be?"

"The country? Hmmm . . . that's a little out of my jurisdiction," she said, "but let me ask a few questions. How far out in the country? Is it toward the mountains or toward the ocean?"

The lost birds looked at each other, feeling really lost.

"We don't know!" explained Jake. "We got trapped in Mr. Walter's milk truck, in the dark, and ended up here."

"Hmmm . . . that's not much to go on," said the mare. "But I will check with my sources and see if anyone has heard of this 'Grandma Daisy.'" She perked up her ears. "My ride's coming. I'll have to get back to you."

Then a man dressed in blue wearing a funny hat, walked out of a small building nearby, hopped up on her back, and they rode off.

For the first time . . .

Jake and Dogwood began to realize that they might never get home.

Good Save!

For the next four days, Jake and Dogwood slept in the park, making new friends, and asking everyone about the countryside. Few had ever heard of the place they were trying to get home to. Occasionally, they would venture into the city. But they never stayed long. There were so many people, cars, and more kinds of loud noise than they had ever heard in the country.

They saw Penny, Edison, and Theodora almost every day at the lake. A few times, they even saw Ms. Police Horse. But she and her rider always seemed too busy for conversation.

"I don't think going back into the city is a good idea," Dogwood said, running to catch up with Jake. "Especially on the ground. Come on, Jake, it's getting dark. Let's go back now!"

"We can't find anyone to help us in the air," said Jake, walking with determination. "We have already asked everyone who lives in the park. The city will be more quiet at night. There has got to be someone there who can tell us how to get home! You can turn back, but I am going on."

"Well, okie-dokie then. Since you put it that way," said Dogwood. "You need someone to keep you out of trouble. But if the fumes and pollution make me start sneezing again, I'm heading straight back to the park!"

"Okay, okay." Jake jumped up on a fire hydrant for a better view. "I thought I saw some rats playing over there by that drain pipe. If they are as smart as Rhastus

and Sebastian, I'll bet they know where the country is. Let's go see!"

Jake hopped down to the sidewalk, and started across the street.

Suddenly, in the blink of an eye, he felt himself being scooped up in powerful jaws. With the deafening sound of screeching tires still ringing in his ears, Jake opened his eyes and found himself back on the sidewalk. His legs were wobbly. He looked up to see the same face that almost caused him a heart attack when they escaped from Mr. Walter's truck.

"GOOD SAVE!" shouted Dogwood. "That big bus almost turned my friend into roadkill."

"Are you okay?" the big dog asked Jake.

"Yeah, I think so." Jake looked back to check his tail feathers. "Thanks for saving me. You must be Sparky. Penny told us all about you."

"That's me. The one and only." The old fellow shrugged. "Speaking of Penny, she told me that you boys are looking for a way to get back to the country. That's where I come from."

"REALLY?" shouted the birds. "Then you can help us get home?"

"Seems to me, all you need to do is sneak back into Mr. Walter's delivery truck, and catch a ride home," said Sparky.

Jake and Dogwood looked at each other.

"Now there's a thought. Why didn't we think of that?" said Jake, amazed at how simple it was.

"Do you know what day of the week he goes out there?" asked Sparky, lying down by an alleyway.

"Mondays!" exclaimed his new feathered friends. "What's today?" they asked with growing excitement.

"I believe it's Thursday." They all started counting back. "No, it's Saturday," Sparky concluded.

"So then," cooed Dogwood. "All we have to do is, hide under the dairy loading platform on tomorrow night, and sneak into the truck Monday morning! Coo, woo, coo!" He started puffing up his neck and bobbing his head.

"What's wrong with your friend?" Sparky asked Jake.

"Nothing. He does that when he gets excited," explained Jake. "You should've seen him last Christmas. We gave him a whole bag of safflower seeds. He cooed and puffed up so much, I thought his head was going to explode!"

"Bar har har!" Sparky laughed, imagining the sight.

"Guffaw, snort," joined in Jake.

"Coo coo!" continued Dogwood.

Just then, a roly-poly raccoon came scurrying out from the side alleyway.

"Sparky, Jake, Dogwood!" panted the raccoon. "Where have you guys been? I have been looking all over for you."

"Hey, Gus!" said Sparky, still chuckling. "We're just taking in the night life. What's up?"

"It's Penny, man!" said Gus, in a serious tone. "She's been hurt! Edison and Theodora asked me to spread the word to all her friends for help!"

"PENNY?" asked all three.

"What happened?" asked Sparky, jumping to his feet.

"I saw the whole thing!" declared Gus. "It happened at sunset. She was flying fast, chasing a dragonfly. They went sailing around the corner of a building. The dragonfly escaped through a partly opened window, and Penny couldn't stop in time. She hit the window, then fell hard to the ground."

"Where is she now?" asked Jake.

"Some humans put her in a blanket. I heard them mention the Wood Lake Zoo," Gus replied sadly. "We don't even know if she is still alive."

"The Wood Lake Zoo," said Sparky, thinking out loud. "Yes, I know where that is, and I'm going to go there."

"Zoo?" asked Jake.

"What is a 'zoo'?" finished Dogwood.

"It's a place where humans keep birds and animals on display for show and tell," said Gus, standing up on his hind legs. "They can't be free like us."

"He's right," said Sparky. "But SOME aren't as bad as they used to be. When I was a pup, my human family used to take me there with them." He raised his nose into the air, as if remembering the smell.

"All the animals were kept in such small cages. The monkeys used to throw dung at us, through the bars of their cages. It was such a nasty place. Now they at least give them more space, and natural surroundings." He started walking down the sidewalk, toward the zoo.

"We want to come, too!" shouted Jake and Dogwood, lining up to follow the old dog.

"What about the dairy? If you miss the truck Monday morning, you will have to wait another week to try again," called Sparky over his shoulder.

"We have two nights and a day," said Jake, continuing to follow.

"Yeah, and if we miss the truck Monday, . . . well, she's our friend too, and we want to go with you," chimed in Dogwood.

"Wait for me!" chittered Gus, hobbling along to bring up the rear.

They trooped off down the street in silence. They didn't know where this journey would take them. They only knew that their friend was in trouble, and they had to help.

Zoo News

A tinge of pink sky was showing at the edge of the African Savannah. The tall giraffes were dark outlines in the faint light, making them look like paper cutouts. A variety of bird and animal noises began to increase, as they always did at the first hint of morning.

Over at the patas' mound, the sleepy inhabitants were stirring around and chittering to each other. One by one, the golden-colored monkeys scampered up from their burrows to begin the day.

"Hold still!" Norman, an old male, was preening his mate, Reba. "There's one more behind your ear."

Reba crinkled up her small dark face. "Need some help?" She then began wiggling her tiny ears back and forth. "Come out, you tasty little morsel!"

"Got it" Norman snagged and quickly popped the flea into his mouth.

"GAG ME!" came a voice from the pampas grass nearby. A small field mouse hopped out to greet them. "With all the fruit and good stuff they feed you here, why do you still eat those beastly things?"

"Good morning, Sophie!" They both scampered over to the mouse.

"We haven't seen you in a while. What's the news?"

"First things first," said the little rodent, sitting back on her hind legs.

"Of course," said Reba, who produced a piece of guava from the previous night's dinner. Then the patas curled themselves up to listen.

Sophie quickly ate the fruit and cleaned her whiskers. Then, above the distant sound of lions roaring, hyenas laughing, and elephants trumpeting, she told them all the latest "zoo" news.

It seems the new orangutan home was almost finished. They just needed to put in a huge waterfall, and install the treetop climbing hammocks. The brown bear cubs were doing well. An eighteen-foot python was regaining his appetite, after unwisely swallowing a light bulb. The ocelot had a healthy baby girl, who was doing fine. One of the old grey parrots had to have cataract surgery to save his eyesight. The temperature control in the tropical rainforest went haywire, but was quickly

repaired before any exotic birds could be turned into popsicles.

Finally, the Humboldt penguins were feeling much better. It seems Calvin, the green-crested basilisk, managed to get into the penguins' habitat. He had a blast skitting across the top of their pond from side to side. The more they squealed, the more he skitted.

"Wow, that would be a scary sight!" Norman laughed. "Can you imagine? Happily sitting there eating a sardine, when this big green lizard goes whizzing past on top of the water?"

"Yeah, they weren't very calm about it." Sophie chuckled, downing one last piece of fruit. "Penguins are birds who can't fly, but I bet they wish they could've flown the coop."

"Oh yeah, speaking of birds . . ." Sophie hopped over to a nearby hedge. "I heard there was an injured falcon brought to the raptor house last night. Word is, she flew into a window."

"Ouch!" Reba grimaced. "Is she going to be alright?"

"Don't know," answered Sophie, checking out her usual departure route. "Peregrine falcons are the fastest animals on earth. They can fly in a dive at speeds up to 175 miles per hour. I'm sure she wasn't going that fast, or she would be taking a mud nap now, as the crocodile says."

"Raptor house?" Norman was confused.

"Oh, Norman, try to keep up. You know . . ." Reba explained. "The place where the caretakers bring large birds, who are sick or injured. Remember?"

"Oh, yeah!" Norman was nodding. "That's where they fix up all the bald eagles and set them free again, right?"

"Right!" said Sophie. "Now, help me up to that branch please. I still have the zebras to see. Hope they had barley for dinner."

"Okay, see you next week!" Norman wrapped his long, skinny tail around her for a hoist up the bush. Then she vanished as quickly as she had arrived.

"How does she know so much?" Norman was scratching his head.

"For as long as I can remember, Sophie has brought us news of the other creatures, in exchange for food," answered Reba. "She learns a lot, and the food is better than rummaging through dumpsters."

"True," said Norman, wrinkling up his nose.

"Speaking of food, it's my turn to groom you!" She reached over and started combing through his hair, in search of tiny delicacies.

So began another day at Wood Lake Zoo.

High Road, Low Road

"WOW!" said Jake.

They had traveled all night and finally stood on a hill overlooking Wood Lake Zoo.

"It looks like the park, only better!" said Dogwood.

"It looks like the country, only better!" joined in Sparky.

"When do we eat!?" Gus sighed. He was lying on

his back with his paws stretched out. "I bet I lost twelve pounds getting here." He raised his head enough to peek down at his rounded belly. "Oh yeah, at least twelve pounds."

"I don't think you are in any danger of being blown away with the next puff of wind," Sparky laughed. "But we're all tired. Let's rest here for a while. We can go down later and find food and water inside." Then he dropped to the ground, put his head down on his front paws, and went fast to sleep.

"Not a bad idea." Jake was flexing his feet. "But I need to sit on a branch."

"No kidding!" agreed Dogwood, stretching his toes. "All this walking has given me a bad case of flat foot. Follow me!"

They both flew over to a rhododendron bush, and tucked their heads under their wings for a quick snooze.

Later that morning, refreshed and eager to move on, the foursome made its way down to a huge grove of trees. There was so much foliage and vegetation, it was hard to know where to begin.

"I've never seen anything like this," Jake was saying, pointing to clusters of burgundy-colored lilies growing by the trail.

It was magnificent, they all agreed, and quietly stood for a moment to take it all in. It seems this "zoo" place was surrounded by a wondrous display of shrubs, grasses, trees, and flowers. Most were not like any they had seen before.

"Are you sure we are in the right place?" asked Gus. "This doesn't look so bad."

They could hear the sounds of many voices floating through the air. There were strange calls and familiar cluckings from birds, animals, and creatures of all kinds.

"Yeah, this is the right place. I told you that SOME 'zoos' have changed, didn't I?" answered Sparky. "Okay, guys, here's the plan. We all split up and look for Penny."

"Good idea," said the other three, nodding their heads.

"Jake and Dogwood, you take the high road. Gus and I will take the low road," Sparky instructed.

"High road?" asked Dogwood.

"Yeah, the high road. You know, the sky . . . the blue yonder . . . the air," explained Sparky. "Fly overhead and see what you can find."

"Whoever finds Penny first, stay with her until the rest of us catch up. Agreed?" asked Sparky, checking with each of the others.

"Okay then, let's get going! I'm sure I smell hot dogs up there!" The old dog headed up the trail, following his nose.

"Sniff . . . smells more like tacos to me!" said Gus, as he scampered down the opposite trail, with renewed enthusiasm. "Good luck, boys!"

Dogwood looked over at Jake. "Okie-dokie, then."

"Hey, you're not afraid are you?" asked Jake.

"Heck no! . . . Well, maybe just a little." Dogwood scuffed at the dirt with his toe. "We don't know what creatures are in there."

"Yeah, I know what you're saying," said Jake,

trying to sound reassuring. "But just think of this as another one of our great adventures!"

"I've had about all the ADVENTURE I can stand for one week," replied Dogwood, shaking his head. "When we get home, I'm going to sleep for a week, and not leave the house even once."

"Sounds good!" Jake nodded. "I might even eat a double helping of Grandma Daisy's tofu sunflowers!"

"Ugh, let's not go that far." Dogwood laughed, feeling better. "Hey! I see some juicy-looking berries on that bush over there. What do you say we have lunch before hitting the high road?"

"I'm there, buddy!" Jake laughed. They both flew over to sample the local fare, still joking around about home, and what everyone was doing there. They felt sure it would not be long before they would see them again, and that gave them courage to take the high road.

The Raptor House

"Mama?"

Penny opened her eyes and looked around. There were white ceilings and sunshine filtering through a window to the side. *What was this place?* She closed her eyes again, trying to remember.

"Best not to move much at first," came an unfamiliar voice.

Penny blinked her eyes in the direction of that

voice until she was able to focus. Sitting on a wooden perch a few feet away was a large bald eagle.

"Glad you're finally awake!" boomed the eagle. "Not much company around here these days. By the way, my name is Petie. Well, Peter that is, but everyone calls me Petie. What is your name, young lady?"

Penny looked down at her wings. They were wrapped in strange material. She was lying on her back and didn't seem to be able to move.

"Oh, sorry!" said the eagle. "Didn't mean to go on like that. How are you feeling?"

No answer.

"Well, I'm sure you probably just want to rest." Petie stretched his wings and bobbed his fearsome-looking head.

Penny tried to move her talons. "Ow!" she cried.

"Hey there, take it easy now!" called Petie. "You got yourself busted up pretty good. The caretakers are doing the best they can to help you get well."

"The caretakers?" she asked.

"Oh, she does know how to speak!" teased the eagle. "Now, what did you say your name was?"

"Penny . . . mmm . . . headache." She grimaced.

"Your name is Penny Headache?"

"No . . ." Penny couldn't help giggling. "My name is Penny and I HAVE a headache."

"Well, Penny is a nice name and you have a nice laugh," chuckled Petie. "Gregory is going to like you. He is most anxious to talk to you. He has been the only one of his kind here, until now."

"Who is Gregory, who are the caretakers, where

am I, how did I get here, how long have I been here, and what happened to me?" jabbered Penny, trying not to sound hysterical.

"Okay, just calm down," said the eagle. "Geez, you sound like one of those reporters who are always talking on TV. You know . . . who, what, where, when, and all that newspaper stuff."

"So, you know about that?" she asked, giving him a piercing look.

"Who doesn't?" Petie answered, with a shrug to fluff his feathers. "Anyway, it's natural to have lots of questions. I did when I was first brought here five years ago. I had been shot in the leg and the bone was shattered. I was young like you, and I got lucky, because they brought me here—"

"Petie!" she interrupted.

"What?" he asked, genuinely puzzled.

"Do you always talk so much without breathing? How do you do that? Never mind . . . please, tell me who the caretakers are."

Petie swiveled his head and took a deep breath. "The caretakers are humans who care about birds, plants, animals, and all living things."

He stopped, looked at Penny, then took another breath.

"They have helped many injured birds like us, get well and return to the wild. Some, like me, are not able to go back, because they would not be able to care for themselves. So they live here."

Penny and Petie continued to talk for most of the afternoon. He filled her in on what he knew of her

accident and how she got there. She managed to roll over and get to her feet, and was not sitting on her own perch.

"Okay, so now tell me about this Gregory," said Penny, sipping water from a nearby tray.

"Gregory is a peregrine falcon who was brought here last year as part of a family redevelopment project," explained Petie.

"Redevelopment for the peregrine family?" she asked.

"Exactly!" Petie reached down to scratch his beak on the wooden perch. "I don't understand it all, but I guess many falcons were affected by something called pesticides."

"Pesticides? Hmmm, go on," she said.

"Well, I guess it's not used much anymore. Thanks to people like the caretakers," continued Petie. "But during the time that farmers used it in their fields to get rid of plant-eating bugs, it had a bad result for the peregrines, and others."

Petie slowed down, and took a deep breath. Then he went on. "It made the shells of peregrine eggs so fragile and thin, that the eggs broke open before the chicks were large enough to live on their own. Many did not survive."

Penny nodded her head, vaguely remembering these stories from her parents.

"Gregory was one of those few who did," explained Petie. "Now, in this safe place, the caretakers want to help him become a daddy, so more falcons can be born to help preserve the family. Cool, huh?"

"That sounds good," said Penny, thinking of the fate of her own family.

"Yeah, except there have not been any female falcons available . . . until now." Petie was bobbing his head with approval.

"The wedding will be glorious. I get to be best man. Everyone will celebrate. There will be lots of reporters. Maybe I will even get my picture on TV, like you. There will be lots of children, and grandchildren . . ."

"Whoa, wait just a minute!" shouted Penny. "Marriage, children, are you talking about me? Not in your lifetime, you old bird. Has anyone ever told you how pushy you can be? I have no intention of marrying anyone! Check, please! I want to go home!"

"Calm down, didn't mean to get you upset," chirped Petie, feeling quite cheerful and happy with himself. "Don't forget to breathe!"

"I have a life in the city! I have friends!" said Penny. "I have adopted parents. I want to go back! Besides, I bet I won't even like him!"

"Who, Gregory?" asked Petie, lifting one eyebrow. "Don't be silly; everyone likes Gregory. You're just cranky because you have a headache. You better get some more sleep. The caretakers will be in to check on you soon. I'm sure they will be glad to see that the future Mrs. Gregory is improving."

"Cut that out!" shrilled Penny. "I'm quite sure I won't like him! Now, if you can manage to be quiet for five minutes, I would like to rest."

"That's a good idea," agreed Petie. "Gregory will

be back from his exercising soon. You really should try to be in a better mood!"

"Oh, you are impossible!" Penny exclaimed.

First, she tried to put her head under her right wing. It hurt. Then she tried to put her head under her left wing. That didn't feel good either. Then she fluffed up her feathers as best she could, let out a long sigh, turned her head away from Petie, and closed her eyes.

Hark! Who Goes There?

"Toto, we're not in Kansas anymore," Jake was muttering to himself.

He and Dogwood had separated to find Penny. Now, he was sitting in a tree surrounded by vines and draping moss.

"Strange critters all over the place, so just go up and ask someone." He kept talking to himself, trying to muster up courage.

"Have you seen Penny the Falcon?" he rehearsed to himself.

From his viewpoint, he could see several different animals. Some were familiar, some not. He looked around for the friendliest face.

To the far left, he had been watching an amazing sight. There were several monkey-like creatures, with white beards. They appeared to be wearing baseball caps, and they were throwing themselves wildly from bush to bush.

"Maybe they should switch to decaf," Jake

muttered, then turned to see who else he might approach.

Directly underneath his tree, sat a gorilla. He at least seemed more relaxed. Jake watched him for a while.

The big fellow was holding a stubby piece of wood on his lap. The dead branch had holes in it, and the gorilla kept poking his little finger into the holes.

Hmmm . . . either he is looking for food, or he's making up a new board game, thought Jake.

"So, these are my choices," Jake continued out loud. "Looks like I have the baseball bush jumpers over there, or King Kong down below . . . What's a fellow to do?"

"Depends," came a voice from behind.

Jake turned around, but couldn't see anything through the green maze.

"Hark! Who goes there? Friend or foe!" he called out, still in a teasing mood after his lunch with Dogwood.

"FRIEND of course!" came the response.

"Then, show yourself or bare the blade of my sword!" ordered Jake, using his best Shakespearean accent.

"HERE!" said the creature, bobbing his head, so Jake could see the movement.

Jake flew over to get a closer look. He couldn't believe his eyes. There sat what appeared to be a large bird. It had furry-looking feathers, large yellow eyes, and some SERIOUS eyebrows. They were huge, fuzzy, and BLUE.

"What planet are you from?" asked Jake.

"Earth, of course," laughed the bird. "My name is Avery, and I am a plush-crested jaybird."

Jake moved over to take a closer look.

"Are those eyebrows for real, or do you put them on with velcro or something?" asked Jake, trying not to stare.

"Cah wah ha!" laughed Avery. "They are real, indeed! Welcome to my world. You seemed a little lost. I thought I might be able to help."

"Okay, great!" said Jake. "But first, maybe you can explain about those guys." Jake pointed to the far left.

"The Guenons?" asked the jay. "They are a curious bunch, aren't they? They are monkeys who travel through the jungle by jumping across clumps of foliage. It may look clumsy, but they can travel very fast. Like many of us here, they come from the tropical rainforests of Africa."

"Africa? Really?" Jake scratched his head. "According to Grandma Daisy's geography lessons, that would be on the other side of the world. What are you doing here?"

"Heck, I was born here!" said Avery, swiveling his head. "However, there are many birds and animals who live there, and the tropical rainforests of Africa are in danger of disappearing. We are being joined by the caretakers to prevent this disaster, if possible."

"I've heard about the caretakers," said Jake. "They sound like good humans. I hope they can help you get normal eyebrows."

"Cah wah ha!" laughed Avery. "Why, so I can be a

bald face like you?" He laughed even louder. "So now, my friend, how can I help you find your way?"

"I'm looking for a friend of mine who was brought here last night," Jake explained. "Her name is Penny, and she is a peregrine falcon. Do you know where she might be?"

"The famous peregrine falcon who was born on the universal skyscraper?" asked Avery.

"That would be the one. What have you heard?"

"This is very exciting. Sophie told us all about her. She didn't know how famous this falcon was, at first. We all hope she will be alright, and that her injuries will heal."

"Sophie?" asked Jake. "Oh, never mind. I don't have much time. I have a milk truck to catch in the morning. Just tell me where I can find her. Please!"

"Hark! No problem! She would be at the Raptor House," said Avery. Then he raised his fuzzy blue eyebrows up and down several times. He turned his head, and pointed to the west.

Cousins?

"That mountain goat didn't have to be so rude." Gus was fussing as he made his way across a log bridge. "He didn't even give me a chance to ask about Penny."

Suddenly, there was a loud squealing, stampeding noise to his left.

"Yeow!" Gus jumped up, then tried to keep his

hold on the log. No luck. He slipped off and fell a short distance to the water below.

"SPALASH!" came the sound as the portly raccoon landed in the pool. He swam to the edge, climbed up, and shook himself off, muttering, "Great, great . . . just great, geez . . . hope that mountain goat wasn't watching."

"Uh, . . . uhyuh. That was uh . . . pretty entertaining."

"What?" said Gus, shaking the water out of his ear. "Somebody say something?"

"Uh, yeah . . . uh, that would be me," came a low, hesitant voice.

Gus looked around. There he was. A turtle sitting by the water with his head barely visible.

"Hi, fella! My name is Gus. Come on out! It's okay, don't be shy."

"Uh, I'm not shy . . . uh, I'm actually, uh . . . very outgoing," said the turtle, reaching his head out farther. "Uh, I'm a sidekick turtle . . . uh, name's . . . uh, Lightning."

"Lightning? Named for your quick wit, not your speed, right?" Gus laughed and winked at the little fellow.

"Uh, yukity," chortled the turtle. "Nope, . . . neither one. Uh, . . . had something to do, . . . uh . . . with the yellow stripes on my face." He stuck his head out farther to demonstrate.

"Pretty impressive," said Gus, admiring the yellow design. "Hey, Lightning. Who made that loud noise anyway?"

"Uh, don't know . . . been hearin' it . . . uh, about every day now . . . but, uh, don't know who," answered the turtle, pulling his head back in. "Well, uh . . . nice meetin' ya. Uh, gotta go back to sleep now."

"Wait, I want to ask you about my friend Penny." Gus stuck his nose down to peek in, but Lightning was out for the night.

"Maybe my mom could help!" The young voice came from overhead.

Gus looked up to see a monkey. No, it wasn't . . . well, maybe. It had big brown eyes, a small face, tiny ears, and a ringed tail. Just like his.

"Hey," called Gus. "Are you a cousin of mine or something?"

"I'm a lemur monkey," said the young one. "What are you?"

"I am a raccoon," stated Gus with pride. "Hmmm . . . raccoons and monkeys related. Why not? I'm told monkeys are related to everyone else."

"My name is Daniel. Follow me!" He jumped over, down and up again. "We'll find my mom. She can help you. She knows everything."

An hour later, Gus came huffing into a clearing. He was sure he had lost the little primate. There had been no sign of him since the stream.

"What took you so long?"

Gus looked up. There, on a branch sitting side by side, were three lemur monkeys. Daniel on one side, with his medium-ringed tail hanging down. Mom in the middle, with her long-ringed tail hanging down. Then, baby lemur on the other side, with a tiny-ringed tail

hanging down. It looked funny, and if Gus hadn't been so tired and hungry, he probably would've had a good laugh.

"Daniel, quiet now," scolded Mom, then said to Gus, "Daniel is a good boy, but sometimes he forgets his manners. My name is Angela, and this is baby Mackenzie. Daniel says you have questions. How can we help?"

"Well, I bet you don't have any french fries or tacos around here, do ya?"

"No." Angela smiled charmingly. "I don't even know what those things are."

"FOOD!" said Gus. "Oh, . . . sorry. Didn't mean to bellow like that. It's been a long day."

"Food, of course," she said. "We were just about to have dinner. Won't you join us?"

Later, they all sat around a huge stump that was covered with various fruit, roots, and vegetables. Poor Gus, not a french fry in sight.

"I don't like papaya!" Daniel was saying. "I want french fries and tocas, too."

"That would be TACOS," corrected Gus, sighing, as he nibbled a piece of kiwi. "Daniel here said that you know everything, and that you can answer my questions."

"I DO know everything. I'm a mom," Angela said with a straight face. "Ask, and I shall tell."

"First, what was that ear-piercing noise that made me lose my balance and fall into the pond?" asked Gus, going for a ginger root.

“He means the Malayans,” explained Daniel, giving her a knowing look.

“Oh.” Angela nodded her head. She went on to explain about the monkeys being moved into their new home. A big new home, with lots of forest to explore.

“This is a bad thing?” asked Gus.

“No, it’s great,” she said, using her tail to wipe bananas from the baby’s face. “But these creatures were born and raised in a small cage. All this new freedom is a learning thing for them. They have to learn to trust. So, at least once a day, they get up the courage to go rampaging around the forest of their new home.”

“I see,” said Gus. “So, they make all this mind-boggling noise, as they run about, to shout their independence, and warn off any possible dangers.”

“Something like that.” She smiled and curled her tail around the children.

“Okay, next question. Are you ready?” joked Gus. “This is the big one.”

“He wants to know about the falcon,” said Daniel.

Gus looked over his shoulder and back again. “How did you know that?”

“Everyone knows,” said Daniel, shrugging his shoulders. “We have ways of getting news about everything.”

“Why are you looking for this famous falcon?” asked Angela.

“My friends and I came here to find her and bring her back to the park where we all live,” explained Gus.

“That’s interesting.” She smiled. “I would think

after she gets married to Gregory, that she would want to stay here."

"What? Married . . . what are you talking about? Don't answer that, I don't want to know. Just tell me where she is, I must talk to her!" shouted Gus.

"You will find her at the Raptor House." Angela pointed to the south. "Daniel can take you to the edge of our home and give you directions from there. Good luck. Maybe we will see you again at the wedding."

"This is amazing," Gus frumped. "Fly in the park one day, hit a window, go to the zoo, get married the next day. Only Penny could do something like that. Let's go, Daniel, lead the way."

They trooped down the trail. One thin ringed tail followed by a bushy one.

Cupid's Arrow

The Raptor House was dark, except for a few rays of twilight that filtered through the window. Eerie shadows fell across the floor, signaling an end to another day at the zoo.

Penny's eyes were still closed. She was slowly awakening from her sleep. She felt a presence . . . someone close by.

She thought, *If I don't open my eyes, I can pretend that this has all been a dream.*

"Ahem . . ."

Who was that? she thought. *Didn't sound like*

Petie. It must be that Gregory fella. Okay, I might as well face him and get it over with.

Penny slowly opened one eye, and peeked around. There was someone sitting next to her.

"Oh, sorry. Hope I didn't wake you."

Penny opened both eyes. This was definitely not Petie. She swiveled her head to get a better look.

Just then, soft light filled the corners of the Raptor House. She found herself looking at the most handsome creature she had ever seen. Her heart was beating faster.

"What kind of experience is this?" she asked.

"Oh, those are just the automatic lights. Welcome back!" boomed Petie. "You have been sleeping all day. The caretakers removed one bandage, but left the other one on because they didn't want to wake you." Then, he stopped. The two falcons weren't listening.

"Oh, yeah! I believe introductions are in order." Petie bobbed his head. "Penny, meet Gregory. Gregory, this is Penny."

"Hello," said Gregory.

Penny's heart was fluttering and her knees had a funny, weak feeling. *Must be a result of my injury,* she thought. Yet, every time she looked into that proud and handsome falcon face, she felt strange.

"How are you feeling?" He was concerned.

"Fine," she managed. "Really, . . . much better now. When can I go home?"

"Oh, there's plenty of time to talk about that!" answered Petie. "Right now, we have planned a celebration!"

"Celebration? For what?" Penny asked with suspicion.

"We want to celebrate that such a beautiful and famous falcon escaped this accident without major injury," offered Gregory, bowing in her direction.

"Oh . . ." said Penny. There was that fluttering again. "That's nice, thank you."

"We know you must be hungry. It's important to keep up your strength." Gregory flew down to the floor.

There, underneath the window, her new feathered friends had laid out a fine dinner feast, complete with candles and flowers.

"French fries?" Penny asked hopefully.

Suddenly, she was feeling very hungry. She tried to raise her wings for the glide down to the floor, but found it painful.

"Here, allow me." Gregory was back at her side in a flash. "Hold onto my neck."

Penny used her free wing to hold on. They swooped down to join Petie. They lit the candles and began their elegant supper. Soon, they were laughing and sharing stories like old friends.

Time passed, and with little notice, rays of moonlight filtered in . . . to mingle with the candlelight.

Courage Will Prevail

Sparky stood on top of a large log, looking out at the forest.

I'm sure that snowy owl said the Raptor House

was in this direction, but I seem to be lost, the old dog was thinking.

"Glad to hear the news that she's okay," he muttered out loud. "After I give Penny a big hug, I'm going to make her promise not to chase dragonflies ever again. Wait . . . what was that sound?"

Sparky's neck hair began to stiffen. He scanned the forest, ears alert. The full moon gave everything a ghostly appearance. Then to the left, . . . movement.

Without taking his eyes away, Sparky stepped to the ground. At a distance of about twenty yards, he could see the outline of a huge grey wolf.

Doesn't look like he's in the mood to exchange business cards, thought the old dog. *Since I seem to be lost anyway, I guess there's no harm in taking a little short cut.* Then he quickly moved toward a nearby ravine.

Later, Sparky was making his way through the woods, safely away from any canine confrontation, when he heard the unmistakable sound of frogs croaking.

"Great! There must be water ahead. I'm thirsty." He moved toward their calls.

Finally, Sparky came to the edge of a small pond. He put his head down and drank his fill.

"Ahhh . . . burp." He looked around, aware that frogs were gathering close by.

"Hey! Didn't I see you guys in that Superbowl commercial?" joked the old fellow.

"Nah, those were our cousins," came a throaty answer.

"Really? Hey, guys . . ." Sparky stepped forward to get a better look. He asked for directions to the Raptor House and was quite relieved he had not strayed too far off course. Then he realized there were only three frogs. That seemed odd.

"Where's all your friends?" Sparky asked, remembering the pond on his childhood farm. There were thousands of frog voices that could be heard every spring. He loved the sound. It meant that winter was over and summer was just ahead.

"Ribbet! Not that many of us left," the frogs chorused. "Many of our cousins are much worse off. Bad things in the environment, they say . . . Ribbet!"

That neck hair was getting stiff again. Partly, because of a wary sense the wise old dog had about the changes he had seen during his years. He knew the threads of all life were woven together in a delicate fabric. One by one, the strands were being pulled on the blanket that protects all things.

"We need to mend our ways, before we unravel it all," Sparky shouted at the top of his lungs.

But mostly his neck hair was straight up because he had been aware of the gray wolf moving in the shadows.

Exit, stage left! the lab was thinking. Then suddenly, the wolf moved in for the kill.

"GRRRR . . . Growl!" The wolf bared his fangs. To Sparky, they appeared to be a foot long. The beast leveled them all with his yellowed-eyed glare and blood-wrenching snarls. He moved closer to his target.

"Going in my sleep was more what I had in mind," said Sparky.

The wolf was only a few feet away now. His mouth drooled, and his white fangs glistened in the moonlight.

"OKAY, YOU OVERGROWN BULLY!" shouted Sparky, stepping forward. "I'm here to rescue my friend, and I'm not letting a puffed-up ball of hot air like you stop me!!"

Suddenly, the wolf froze. He whimpered and backed away. Then he turned and ran, whining louder with every step.

"Well, that's more like it . . ." Sparky said, his knees shaking. "Did you see that?" He stuck out his chest. "Just goes to show that courage will always prevail! Good luck, guys! I must continue my journey now." And away he went, with his head held high.

"Hey, Dudley!" croaked the three frogs. "You showed up for our game just in time to scare off that wolf again. Too bad you didn't get a chance to meet our new friend."

"Yeah, too bad," said the porcupine, waddling over. "Darts, anyone?"

Here Kitty, Kitty

"Ahhh . . . a nice bath is just what I need to get rid of the road dust," Dogwood announced cheerfully to himself.

He was alone in the moonlight, splashing wildly at the edge of a small pond. There was a slight waterfall

spilling into the pool, which made for a great birdbath and shower.

He finished, and flew up to a nearby rock to fluff and dry.

"I want to look my best when I see Penny at the Raptor House," said Dogwood, flapping and fluffing. "Which is just at the top of this hill."

He could see the outline of a house. There was faint light glowing from the windows.

I'm excited to see Penny and meet up with the others, he was thinking. *The hyenas I talked to said she wasn't badly hurt. I can't wait to exchange stories with the guys. Everyone I met today was friendly and helpful.* He laughed out loud, thinking about his earlier fear of strange zoo creatures.

A short time later, Dogwood was foofed, preened, fluffed, dried, and ready to go see Penny.

"Well, I may not be the first to find her, but I bet I'll be the cleanest." He moved up to a large boulder to get a better look at his destination.

He was just getting ready to spring into the air, when a huge paw came out of nowhere and stomped on his tail. Dogwood looked back to see a large cat leering overhead. Amazingly, the dove had no fear of becoming the cat's midnight snack.

In fact, Dogwood was greatly annoyed.

"LOOK WHAT YOU DID TO MY TAIL!" squawked the bird, pulling himself free. "I just spent a lot of time getting my feathers all shiny white and clean! Look what you did!" Dogwood paraded around in a circle, fluffing to shake off the damage.

"RRRRR . . . RRR . . . ROAR!!" blasted the cat.

Dogwood stood facing him. His feathers were being blown by the cat's windy bellows.

"Well, okay then . . . thank you," said Dogwood, flicking off one last speck of dust from his tail. "That helped me get clean again. All is forgiven."

The fearsome creature narrowed his eyes and licked his lips.

"Gulp," Dogwood swallowed nervously. "By the way, I'm Dogwood, friend of Penny the falcon." That statement helped him make new friends all day.

But the cat didn't seem impressed. He paced back and forth, trying to decide what to do.

"Well, maybe you haven't heard of Penny yet. But that's okay. Actually, I like cats. One of my best friends is a cat," said Dogwood, thinking of Styles at home.

The cat stopped and turned toward the bird. His tail twitched. A decision had been made. He took a step forward . . .

"Livingston!"

A small mouse hopped into the middle and sat halfway between them. "Not a particularly good idea!"

The cat lowered his head, thought about it, growled once more, then walked back into his cave.

"Sophie?" asked Dogwood. "You're the zoo resident news broadcaster I've heard about all day, right? It's a pleasure to meet you."

"Yes, and you must be Dogwood the dove, friend of Penny the falcon." They both smiled, and started chatting about the latest events.

"By the way, Livingston is really a sweetheart, once

you get to know him," explained Sophie. "He's just a little cranky, because the jaguars of his family are endangered and close to becoming extinct."

"You mean like the dinosaurs?" said Dogwood. "That would be a shame."

Suddenly, there was a commotion in the distance.

"FIRE!!" they heard.

"FIRE AT THE RAPTOR HOUSE!"

A Night to Remember

"PENNY!"

Dogwood looked toward the house. He could see flames flickering from the window.

"I know what to do!" Sophie jumped onto Dogwood's back. "Take me over those trees!"

"But that's in the wrong direction!" protested Dogwood.

The voices were growing louder in the distance. Residents of the zoo were awakening to the fire alarm.

"Trust me!" yelled Sophie. "We must go now!"

Dogwood took two steps forward, then launched himself and his passenger into the air. They flew toward the palm trees of the African Savannah.

Meanwhile, Sparky, Gus, and Jake had met up earlier a short distance from the Raptor House. They were approaching the house to find Penny, when they saw the flames. That's when they shouted the "FIRE" alarm.

Now they all stood helplessly outside the window.

Jake hovered high enough to see inside. The curtains were engulfed in flames. Beyond that, he could see three figures huddled in the middle of the room.

"Penny's inside with an eagle and another falcon!" said Jake, going down to give a report to Sparky and Gus. "What can we do to get them out?"

"I tried the front door, but the caretakers have it locked!" said Sparky.

"We need to break the window!" chittered Gus.

"We need to get water!" squawked Jake.

Then they were all suddenly quiet. They looked at the ground. It was vibrating under their feet. Small pebbles and pine needles were bouncing up and down, like Mexican jumping beans.

"Oh, great!" said Jake. "Is it an earthquake? Just what we need! With a little luck, the house will topple on us all. The good news is, the fire will be put out. The bad news is, we'll all be dead!"

"Such a talent for exaggeration! Mind if we help out!?"

"DOGWOOD!" shouted Jake. "That sounds like my buddy, Dogwood!"

They looked up the hill to see an astonishing sight. An elephant the size of a small town, was lumbering their way. The ground trembled with each mighty step. On top of his head sat a small mouse, and their dubious friend, Dogwood.

"Water, Jeremiah! Water!" commanded Sophie.

The elephant plunged his trunk into a huge water-holding tank at the side of the house. He then moved around to the window. At Sophie's command,

he raised a massive foot, and with barely a tap, the window was eliminated.

Without hesitation, Jeremiah sprayed water on the flames. They had spread from the curtains to the wall. The force of the water doused most of the fire. After Jeremiah took one more trip to the tank, the flames were completely gone. It was all over.

Once again, a tinge of pink was framing the outer trees of the zoo and faint voices were beginning to greet another day. It had been a night to remember.

After putting out the fire, Jeremiah had reached in with his long trunk, and gently removed Penny, Gregory, and Petie from harm's way. He was now back at the African Savannah, telling all his friends about the exciting rescue. He was quite a hero.

The event had caused a commotion throughout the zoo. Well-wishers had signaled their messages the remainder of the night.

Many voices had floated across the air, but now all was quiet again. Things were getting back to normal. Everyone was returning to his or her daily routine, and Sophie had returned to spreading the news.

Penny's family of old and new friends sat together near the Raptor House. Gregory had remained close to Penny, and she didn't seem to mind. They all felt very lucky. Other than a broken window, and some charred curtains, there was very little damage.

"Our dinner candle started the fire," said Petie. "One minute we were eating and laughing, then . . . WHOOSH! The flames shot up the curtains. Guess we put our picnic a little too close to the wall."

"Too close, alright," said Sparky. "That would be a good description of the whole night!" Then he told his story about meeting the grey wolf.

Then, just as Gus started telling his story about the Malayans—

"Wait a minute!" shouted Jake, looking at Dogwood. "What time is it?"

"THE MILK TRUCK!" they yelled together.

"It's barely dawn. You can make it if you hurry," encouraged Sparky. "It will be quicker if you fly to Mr. Walter's truck."

"It took us all of Friday night just to get here," said Dogwood. "We followed you. We don't have a clue how to get to the dairy."

"Guess we'll just have to wait until next Monday," said Jake, feeling more homesick than ever.

But then . . .

"I can get you to Mr. Walter's dairy." Ms. Police Horse came trotting down the path. "Heard you fellas had a little excitement here last night. Thought I'd stop by to investigate."

"Holy cow! Are you serious?" Dogwood said, puffing up his neck.

"Don't see any cows around here, just one smart horse," she answered. "Not much time. Jump onto my saddle and hold on to my mane!"

The dove and the starling jumped up and positioned themselves on her back.

"Well, friends, this is good-bye for now!" Jake said, looking down to the faces he had grown to love. "Come to the country sometime for a visit!"

"Penny, we all heard the rumor that you and Gregory are getting married," teased Dogwood. "Is that true?"

The two falcons looked at each other with a knowing smile.

"I need to recover from my injury," she said, blushing. "So let's just say that I will be staying here for a while."

"Okie-dokie then!" said Dogwood, tucking his tail under the saddle horn.

"HIYO SILVER!" shouted Jake. "Take us home!"

With a whinny, and a twitch of her tail, Ms. Police Horse lunged forward in the direction of the rising sun, the dairy truck, and . . . home.

Appendix

Zoo Characters and Honorable Mention

On the return: numbers are gradually increasing.
Preserved: numbers have improved enough to be removed from threatened list.
Threatened: numbers are close to endangered levels.
Endangered: numbers are close to extinction.

Peregrine falcon	on the return
Giraffe	preserved
Golden pata monkeys	threatened
Orangutan	threatened
Brown bears	threatened
Python	preserved
Ocelot	threatened
Exotic birds/African parrots	preserved
Humboldt penguins	preserved
Green-crested basilisk	preserved
Zebras	preserved
Bald eagle	on the return
Gorilla	endangered
Guenon monkeys	endangered
Plush-crested jay	threatened
Mountain goat	preserved

Malayan monkeys	endangered
Sidekick turtle	endangered
Lemur monkeys	endangered
Snowy owl	threatened
Grey wolf	on the return
Frogs (multiple species)	endangered
Porcupines	preserved
Jaguar	endangered
Lions	threatened
African elephant	endangered

**Source:* Woodland Park Zoo, 1995, Seattle, Washington.

MW00907111